Joseph C. Heywood

Salome - The Daughter of Herodias

A Dramatic Poem

Joseph C. Heywood

Salome - The Daughter of Herodias
A Dramatic Poem

ISBN/EAN: 9783337194543

Printed in Europe, USA, Canada, Australia, Japan

Cover: Foto ©Andreas Hilbeck / pixelio.de

More available books at **www.hansebooks.com**

THE DAUGHTER OF HERODIAS.

A DRAMATIC POEM.

NEW YORK:

PUTNAM, 532 BROADWAY.

1862.

M'CREA & MILLER, STEREOTYPERS.   O. A. ALVORD, PRINTER.

" But when Herod's birthday was kept, the daughter of Herodias danced before them, and pleased Herod. Whereupon he promised with an oath to give her whatsoever she would ask. And she, being before instructed of her mother, said, Give me here John the Baptist's head in a charger. And the king was sorry: nevertheless for the oath's sake and them which sat with him at meat, he commanded it to be given her."

SAINT MATTHEW.

SALOME;

OR, THE

DAUGHTER OF HERODIAS.

A DUNGEON.

JOHN BAPTIST *in a trance ; Heaven opened ; the heavenly host gathered before the throne.*

ALL THE HEAVENLY HOST.

Light invisible ;

Light-giving Darkness inscrutable ;

Source unsupplied, Source all-receiving ;

Boundless Duration, that, yearless, endures
    not but still is ;

Sternness unwavering, limitless ; Tenderness
    melting and infinite :

Omnipresent and sleepless Benevolence; Vengeance that sleeps omnipresent;

Ever creating and restless Creator, from finished creation resting forever;

Justice that sees not and feels not; feeling for
all and all-seeing Pity;

Hidden and fathomless Mystery, mysteries
hidden revealing;

Love all-pervading; exhaustless and measure-
less Love;

Love all-conquering; Love all-invincible;

Father of Christ Omnipotent;

Alleluiah!

Glory, majesty, victory and honor be unto
Thee

Forever and ever and ever.

Amen.

A VOICE.

He hath gone to the vineyard alone; is there
no one to help?

ARCHANGELS.

There is none; He must gather alone.

VOICE.

He treadeth the wine-press alone; is there no one to help?

ARCHANGELS.

There is none; He must tread it alone.

VOICE.

He hath gone 'gainst the Dragon alone; is there no one to help?

ARCHANGELS.

There is none; He must conquer alone.

VOICE.

Grief's archers sore press Him alone; is there no one to help?

ARCHANGELS.

There is none; He must suffer alone.

VOICE.

Death's sorrows o'erwhelm Him alone; is there no one to help?

ARCHANGELS.

There is none; He is victor alone.

VOICE.

Hell's legions assail Him alone; is there no
one to help?

ARCHANGELS.

There is none; He shall triumph alone.

ALL THE HEAVENLY HOST.

Alleluiah !

He shall receive

The kingdom, the majesty, the power and the
Glory,

Forever and ever and ever.

Amen.

CHERUBIM.

The worlds, that, circling in their courses, roll,

And with their chariot-wheels shake either
pole;

The suns that in the firmament do shine,

As footsteps of the Architect divine;

Tempests, that, rumbling with a thunder
    sound,
Drive through the air and quake the solid
    ground;
The seas that in their prisons rage and roar,
And foaming oceans chafing 'gainst the shore,
Like fevered giants rolling on their sides,
And madly lashing barriers with their tides;
The new creations from unsparing hand,
Glowing in space and springing from the
    land;
All these thy boundless power and love pro-
    claim,
But Thou in them dost magnify Thy name,
And Thy great glory less, Most Holy One,
Than in the mission of Thy Holy Son.

ALL THE HEAVENLY HOST.

Alleluiah!
Glory and majesty, victory and honor be un-
    to Thee

Forever and ever and ever.

Amen.

SERAPHIM.

Comets that sweep along the lightning's path;
Thy blazing meteor-messengers of wrath;
Rivers of light that flow o'er starry sands
Athwart the heavens to worlds fresh from Thy
    hands,
O'erwhelming with their floods chaotic night,
Fulfilling Thy command "Let there be
    light;"
Torrents of flaming fire, that down the north,
Flow from Thy throne and show Thy glory
    forth;
Winds rushing from their caverns, on the seas
Uplifting mountains; and the gentlest breeze;
The marshalled hosts of storms in upper air
That in wild chorus shout Thy praises there;
And primal colors in their bending frame;
All these Thy might and majesty proclaim,

But magnify Thy name, Most Holy One,
Less than the mission of Thy Holy Son.

ALL THE HEAVENLY HOST.

Alleluiah!
Glory and majesty, victory and honor be unto
   Thee
Forever and ever and ever.
Amen.

A VOICE.

A victor He shall return, and joyful with Him—

ARCHANGELS.

The sorrowful captives of earth.

VOICE.

Triumphant He shall return, and joyful with
   Him—

ARCHANGELS.

The abused and contemned of the Earth.

VOICE.

Almighty He shall return, and joyful with
   Him—

2

ARCHANGELS.

The reviled, for His sake, of the earth.

VOICE.

Avenger He shall return, and joyful with
Him—

ARCHANGELS.

Th' outcasts, for His sake, of the earth.

VOICE.

To judgment He shall return, and joyful with
Him—

ARCHANGELS.

The just, for His sake, of the earth.

VOICE.

Redeemer He shall return, and joyful with
Him—

ARCHANGELS.

His saints, the redeemed of the earth.

ALL THE HEAVENLY HOST.

Alleluiah !
He shall receive

The kingdom, the majesty, the power and the
glory

Forever and ever and ever.

Amen.

Alpha, Omega:

Ancient of Days Eternal;

Hope that is changeless, immortal, life-giv-
ing;

End without any beginning; Beginning that's
endless;

The Abused, the Reviled, the Rejected, the
Mocked, the Accused, the Condemned.

High-Priest self-offered for merciless foes,
bleeding and making atonement;

Friend agonized, interceding; sole Mediator
unfailing; fearful Avenger;

Prince of Peace triumphant o'er all; Lord God
of Sabbaoth;

Pascal Lamb passively suffering; weeping
Christ living forever;

First Thought and Last Thought ; Space filling,
 Heaven-ruling AM ;
Final Hope ; Final Help ; Final Rewarder ;
Messiah, Son of the Father ;
Alleluiah !
Glory, majesty, victory and honor be unto Thee
Forever and ever and ever.
Amen.

ARCHANGELS.

For thou shalt reign—

ALL THE HEAVENLY HOST.

Forever and ever.

ARCHANGELS.

King of kings—

ALL THE HEAVENLY HOST.

Forever and ever.

ARCHANGELS.

And Lord of lords—

ALL THE HEAVENLY HOST.

Forever and ever.

King of kings,
And Lord of lords
For ever and ever,
And ever.
Amen.

The Vision passes.

JOHN BAPTIST.

My work is finished; way made for the Word;
Earth hears in silence Thy approach, O Lord:
The stars from their firm places move aside,
Cerulean gates of Heaven open wide,
The King of Glory from His throne descends,
The darkling age of forms and shadows ends;
He comes to claim among the sons of men
His kingdom; drive th' usurper to his den;
Baptize His subjects with the Holy Ghost,
And seal them members of His heavenly host;
Open the gloomy prisons of the soul,
And set it free from sin's supreme control;
Banish all doubts to everlasting night;

2*

Bring immortality and life to light ;

My work is finished ; way made for the Word ;

Earth trembles 'neath thine awful tread, O
  Lord.

My work is finished ; yet ere I depart

Show me Thyself again, and let my heart,

Filled with Thy certainty, question no more,

But Thee incarnate, doubting naught, adore ;

The mysteries of prophecy unfold,

Realize prophetic visions seen of old,

And let me understand the mighty plan

Regeneration of degenerate man ;

How Thou wilt raise this people, lift their
  horn,

And let them be no more the heathen's scorn,

Avenge them of their foes and bring them
  home,

And safely shelter them from wrath to come ;

Mine hour approaches, give me faith in Thee,

And with the Holy Ghost baptize Thou me;
My work is finished; way made for the Word;
I wait for Thy swift coming, O my Lord.

JESUS.

John Baptist!

. JOHN BAPTIST.

Master, hail! whence comest Thou?

JESUS.

I came not; I am here.

JOHN BAPTIST.

Master and Lord,
Art thou He who should come; or wait we
    still
Another?

JESUS.

I am He.

JOHN BAPTIST.

My Lord and God.

JESUS.

Hereafter thou shalt see upon God's throne

The Son of Man in all His glory sit,
The kingdoms of the earth bowed at His feet,
The universe before His judgment bar.

JOHN BAPTIST.

O then, my Lord and God, remember me.

JESUS.

I will: a good and faithful servant, thou
Into my joy shalt straightway enter.

JOHN BAPTIST.

Lord,
I would commend to Thee those who in faith
Have humbly followed me, looking for Thee.
Reveal Thyself to them, make them Thine own,
Baptize them all with spirit and with fire.

JESUS.

They shall be safely gathered to my fold.

JOHN BAPTIST.

Baptize thou me.

JESUS.

Receive the Holy Ghost.

JOHN BAPTIST. *Alone.*

The Counsellor, Messiah, Prince of Peace,
The Everlasting Father, Mighty God.
The Wonderful, the Son of Man, the Christ.
Now let Thy servant go in peace, O Lord,
For these mine eyes have Thy salvation seen.

Enter Salome.

SALOME.

All hail! good master; from the sentinels
Of fierce intolerance; from my mother's watch,
By stealth and unattended have I 'scaped
To bring thee some refreshment.

JOHN BAPTIST.

Thanks, my child.
I have refreshment that thou knowest not of.
And I am strong in strength sent from on high.
Yet is thy presence balm to the weak parts
Of my humanity.

SALOME.

How went the day?

Laden with tediousness?   Did the light hours
Go crouching down beneath a weight of grief,
Dragging but slowly-on?

JOHN BAPTIST.

The day was not,
Nor were there hours.   Time, for me, is passed.
But now thou callest me back to look on it
In thee.   This is the last.   I must go hence.

SALOME.

Where wilt thou go?

JOHN BAPTIST:

Unto my dwelling-place.

SALOME.

Where is thy home?

JOHN BAPTIST.

On earth 'tis in the hearts
Of those who follow me.

SALOME.

And hast thou one
That is not on the earth?   Where is it then?

JOHN BAPTIST.

'Tis whither thou shalt come.

SALOME.

I'll go with thee.

JOHN BAPTIST.

Thou canst not.

SALOME.

I can all that woman may.
Who will supply thy wants?

JOHN BAPTIST.

I shall have none.

SALOME.

My comprehension cannot grasp thy words;
Where wilt thou go? Thou canst not leave
    this cell,
Unless the king shall please to bid thee forth.

JOHN BAPTIST.

I know thou canst not understand me now,
Thou wilt in time; but this I plainly say,
Thou shalt not listen to my voice again.

SALOME.

Nay, say not so; thou art but sad and faint.

Behold what I have brought; refresh thyself,

Nay, take the wine; and see, how rich these figs!

Wilt thou not let their blushing beauty tempt

Thy lips t' embrace them? Thou canst not
    refuse

These flowers; I saw them smiling in their
    dreams,

And caught them ere they waked; with plead-
    ing look,

And trembling with affright they gaze at me,

Tears glittering on their cheeks, and in their
    eyes.

They too are sad, for they are captives now.

Take fruit and flowers, and then thou wilt not
    say

Thy handmaid shall not visit thee again.

JOHN BAPTIST.

Daughter, I will not eat; but from His throne

Jehovah sees thine offering, to bless
The heart that prompted it.   Yes, I am sad,
My soul's exceeding sorrowful for thee.

SALOME.

For me!   Nay, for thyself; a prisoner thou,
I free as air and happy as the flowers.
But cheer thee, I will try to set thee free.

JOHN BAPTIST.

And thou shalt do it.

SALOME.

Then how I will rejoice!

JOHN BAPTIST.

Nay, thou shalt mourn.

SALOME.

And thou?

JOHN BAPTIST.

I shall rejoice.
At length, thy sorrow shall be turned to joy:
Blessed the sorrowful, they shall rejoice,
And they who mourn, they shall be comforted.

3

SALOME.

Why should I mourn?

JOHN BAPTIST.

For thine eternal good.

SALOME.

Now talkest thou mystery; unfold thyself.

JOHN BAPTIST.

Blessed be they who mourn; lovest thou me?

SALOME.

Thou knowest that I love thee.

JOHN BAPTIST.

Keep my words.

SALOME.

They are enshrined in me.

JOHN BAPTIST.

Lovest thou me?

SALOME.

Now thou dost mock me! must I say again
That I do love thee?

JOHN BAPTIST.

Follow thou the Christ.

SALOME.

Where is He?

JOHN BAPTIST.

He shall come to thee.

SALOME.

I will.

JOHN BAPTIST.

Lovest thou me?

SALOME.

Nay, must I swear to thee?

JOHN BAPTIST.

Follow the Christ, and come whither I go.

SALOME.

Wilt thou not cease to speak in mysteries?

JOHN BAPTIST.

Yea, I will speak no more; have I not said
Thou shalt not listen to my voice again?

SALOME.

'Twas but the wind of jest, that thou might'st see
How strong were my affections grown to thee.
I leave thee now, but take with me thy words;
For, as thou know'st, King Herod with his
    lords
Keeps festival, and in the revelry,
Against my will, I must a sharer be;
But on the morrow I will come to tell
Thee of the feast, and cheer thee in thy cell.
The shadows, trembling, beckon me away:
Jehovah keep thee till the dawn of day.

JOHN BAPTIST.

My daughter, may Jehovah's blessing rest
Forever on thy soul and keep thee pure in
    heart!
And He shall send to thee a Comforter.
Peace be with thee, eternal peace, Christ's
    peace!

Exit Salome.

Lord Jesus, bless this child and bring her home;

I wait Thy coming Lord, O quickly come!

CHORUS, *passing in the street.*

The sun goes down; the day expires—

The color from its deep flushed face

To ash hue pales; the veilèd fires

In slow procession from their place,

The inner court of the great universe,

Come solemnly and spread a pall,

The pall of night, o'er the dead day,

Then lift their veils to watch. O'er all

The moon appears, with steadfast way,

While stars the praises of the lost rehearse,

Mounts up the sky to look upon the sun, and

counts

Him present whom afar she sees, and still

more brightly mounts.

CHORUS OF SPIRITS, *in the air.*

As the sun, so the life of the Son for a time

shall depart;

3*

As the day in the night, so His body be laid
  in the tomb;

As the moon mounteth up to the skies, so
  faith to the heavens,

To see Him, and shine in His beams, and
  know that He liveth.

Like the stars, His Apostles shall watch
  through the dark till He come,

Then shall lose themselves in, and become a
  part of His brightness.

BANQUETING ROOM IN KING HEROD'S PALACE.

King HEROD *and* HERODIAS *seated on thrones.*
Lords, Captains, Courtiers, &c.

FIRST LORD.

THIS is a fair, high day ; King Herod means
We shall have cause to wish him many such.
Didst thou come early to the banquet room ?

SECOND LORD.

Yea, I came in among the very first,
And brightly, swiftly, has the revel sped,
And comet-like, drawn on so fair a train,
So rich a galaxy of beauty, that
Itself is lost to th' eye of contemplation,
In its bright tail increasing to the end.
Dull Satisfaction would await no more,

Did not its guide and mother, Expectation,
Forever hungering, and ne'er content;—
Which it doth follow like a timid child,
But never goes before, nor long time leaves;
Cherish its hunger to a fever, and wait
A course of beauty never yet imagined,
Reserved for delicate palates till the last.

FIRST LORD.

How sayest thou? What then may we ex-
    pect?
For I had thought the richest flowers of earth,
The choicest viands and the sweetest sounds,
From every clime were culled to grace this
    feast.

SECOND LORD.

So all would think, and none would ever
    dream
Of brighter, more enticing loveliness.
Yet here, where winds that saunter through
    the room

Go drunk with music hence, stagger and reel,

Like bacchantes, under festooned garlands

　green;

Where atmosphere is heavy with perfume

From rose-bud lips of every blushing hue,

Carnation cheeks, and waving, lily hands;

A perfume sweeter than arose of yore

From Paradise, or than earth's lips exhaled

In her young, virgin life, ere primal curse;

Here, where the screened and softened, lan-

　guid light

From these rich myriad lamps, whose jewels

　blaze,

And seem themselves to generate the beams,

But serves to show th' alluring, dangerous

　depths

Of dark, dissolving eyes and snowy breasts,

Rolling, like seas, with passions fullest tides;

Here, where the freshest floral wreaths grow

　dim,

Faded by warmth of woman's glowing charms,
Here, where Elysian joys invite the soul
To revel in an ecstasy of bliss,
I waiting stand, unblessed, till I behold,
Transcendent fair, like Venus o'er the wave,
The crowning glory of the feast appear.

Another part of the Room.

FIRST CAPTAIN.

Hast seen this daughter of Herodias?

SECOND CAPTAIN.

I have not; but my memory contains
Rich tales of her surpassing loveliness;
Each tale a mirror, showing each a form,
Each form compact of Fancy's sweetest parts;
Each part, each form, each mirror showing
    naught
But one sweet, changing, changeless, charm-
    ing whole;
As in the mirror of the month is seen
Chaste Dian's phases, Dian still the same.

FIRST CAPTAIN.

Then it were well, if when she doth appear
These forms remain, nor vanish from thy sight,
Leaving thy magic mirrors ugly blanks; ·
And thy chaste Dian fade not from thy skies,
And leave thee groping.

SECOND CAPTAIN.

I myself do fear
Lest I shall lose my sweet divinity,
This image rumor-made within my heart,
Chased from its shrine by hateful verity.

FIRST CAPTAIN.

List! list! the music!—now at length she
comes.

*Folding doors open at the end of the room, and
Salome glides in dancing.*

By all th' immortal gods! I'd swear those
doors
Were of celestial groves the folding gates!
Surely the beauty is Olympian,

Which floats from thence! What features!
 Ah! what form!
What grace! She moves upon the air!

    SECOND CAPTAIN.

        By Jove!
I do believe that some enchantment's here!

    FIRST CAPTAIN.

Look at the King! his fierce, admiring eyes
Devour her every motion. Would'st thou
 think
His head could easy rest upon his couch
This night? Soul-tossing, love-engendered
 dreams,
Will they not drive smiles from his counten-
 ance,
Contentment from his heart, as sails are driv'n
From ships by southern gales, or trees from
 shores
Of islands, by tempestuous, angry waves
That rage upon the great, the midland sea;

And thus his sleep, which bears him through
    the night,
Like a good ship, be wrecked, he left to toss,
And reach the shores of morn, as best he
    may?
By Hercules! if I were but a king,
My kingdom were too small to win the love,
Or e'en possession of that more than queen;
For her I could be Paris!

SECOND CAPTAIN.

        Or Leander?
Hast thou yet heard her voice? Sure it must
    be
Like liquid silver bubbling from its fount
Through a cleft ruby; but she need not speak,
For every action talks with golden tongue.

FIRST CAPTAIN.

Dost note the sad expression of the face:
The downcast, languid eye? She looks as if
She came to dance for pity more than praise;

4

Impelled by sorrow more than vanity.

SECOND CAPTAIN.

Thou readest well. Yet that same saddened
    look,
That unaffected, pleading look contains
A potent charm. She came not willingly ;
It was just now I heard a neighbor say,
That she was very loath to come this night
Before the King: but yet because he wished it,
Obedient also to her mother's will,
She put away her flowing tears and came.

FIRST CAPTAIN.

Why this unwillingness?—and she so fair !
Why hath she never graced the court before ?
Doth modesty abhor, or pride disdain,
And bid her shun with fear, with scorn neglect
Worship gallant, like that which waits her
    here ?

SECOND CAPTAIN.

'Tis said, alone she loves to entertain

Her tender thoughts, and listen to their chants
Of love and all things beautiful.

FIRST CAPTAIN.

Perchance
Hath that keen Subtilty, that cunning wight,
Secured a resting place, where loves do sport,
In that soft vale, 'twixt those twin hillocks
    white,
Whose crested summits nightly blush beneath
The setting rays from those soft-shining orbs,
When they in slumber sink, as sinks the sun
Into mid ocean, at the close of day;
And thence he whispers her ambitious heart
That, if she would have fame, unbounded
    fame,
She should not blind Imagination's sight,
Nor bind its tongue, nor spoil its ready pen,
Nor dull the colors which its pencil spreads
By cold realities, which, Gorgon-like
Turn warm, luxurious Fancy into stone.

SECOND CAPTAIN.

Nay, look again : that tiny, timid ear
Which, frightened, nestles in those heavy locks,
Like frightened dove in the thick foliage
Of a young pine-tree, swaying in the breeze,
Would flee in terror such vile whisperings.

FIRST CAPTAIN.

Then 'tis her mother, who doth strive to make
Her daughter famèd, like the flower which
blooms
But once within its life, a century,
And then, perchance, on such a night as this.

SECOND CAPTAIN.

Her mother may do all, for from her heart
Nature long since, ashamed, did flee away,
And strive in vain to hide its burning blush
'Neath shading lids, or in the bosom's snow
Of her most fair, pure child, yielding its place
To those relentless demon conquerors,
The glittering, armed array of woman's arts.

FIRST CAPTAIN.

With all her woman craft she well must know
That, if the flower's beauty give not fame,
The mystery of its bloom when close conjoint
With fecund wonder, surely will beget
Fame's substance, Rumor, with conjecture
    winged,
And echo-tongued to multiply itself.
Perchance the maiden, in her royal pride,
Would such a flower be, and not for worlds
The violet, beloved and known by all,
Placed in the bosom, carried on the heart;
But sought with curiosity, gazed at
With reverent awe, or spoken of with fear
By none.   Yet she is wondrous beautiful!

SECOND CAPTAIN.

She floats upon the melody, as floats
Earth's richest perfume, dancing on a zephyr!

FIRST CAPTAIN.

Buoyed by her pride and woman's vanity!
    4*

SECOND CAPTAIN.

Thou wrong'st her! In those palaces, from
    which
The rulers of her soul look on the world,
There is no pomp of vanity or pride;
But purest maiden modesty reigns there,
And beauty concentrate of beauties all,
Which takes its form in thought and word
    and act:
Blended in holy harmony, these rule,
While o'er her cheeks their mingling colors
    float,
And wave and rise and fall upon the breeze
Of her heart's gentle breathings.

FIRST CAPTAIN.

                  Since she came
Perforce, to make contentment discontent,
I can forgive her; from this time I see
As seeing not all others of her sex.
I've seen the sun and gazed at it too long;

And now, even in the night, shall see no stars,

But still shall see the sun, the sun, the sun !

Another part of the Room.

FIRST COURTIER.

There is a whisper moving in the air,

Like a faint mist which is and then is not,

Which, even while thou seest, thou wilt think

That thou hast seen it not, seeing no form.

This whisper says, at least it seems to say,

Or this, just now, it seemed to say to me,

Ere I could see 'twas naught, that a high
  place

In the young princess' favor hath been found

By John, whom they surname the Baptist; but

This whisper hath not dared approach the
  queen.

It talks in faintest breathings, lest she hear;

It skulks among the courtiers; but abroad,

Far from the queen, it stalks, in might a
  Stentor;

For well 'tis known Herodias hates the man,
And he now lies in ward at her request.

SECOND COURTIER.

Hast seen this aqueous philosopher?

FIRST COURTIER.

Once: at the even-tide, when the mild air
Had melted me to melancholy thoughts,
Forth from the town I strayed alone and sought
A solitary place where, unobserved,
I could at pleasure humor the strange mood.
In the far west the sun, warm from his course,
Had lain him languid down, and round his
    bed
The blue and golden curtains closely drawn.
An amber mist rose from his smoking coursers,
As they, with drooping necks and heaving
    flanks,
Drunk up the cool west wind and slaked their
    thirst.
Anon, the moon with blushes left her couch,

Where Phebus all the morn had fondled her,

And smiling walked the azure fields of heaven

Among her grazing star-flocks, seeing naught

But that her lord awaits her in the west.

Silence in mid-air listened to the sound

Of music from a choir of far-off spheres,

While Rest stood on the heights, and with her
    wand

Called Slumber down upon the sentient world,

Slumber that, like Penelope, at night

Ravels the web of toil knit through the day.

I turned from gazing on the heavens and saw

This same John Baptist musing, or in prayer.

A bunch of wild-flowers in his half-closed hand

Rested upon his lap ; his look was turned

Toward the Hebrew Temple,. and I thought,

From time to time words issued from his lips.

As I approached he saw me and arose,

And I was led by the sweet dignity

Which draped him, veiling his majestic head,

The placid, manly beauty of his face,
The deep and thrilling tones that on his lips •
Seemed lingeringly to dwell, then heavenward
   went,
The strange, soft light that flooded his deep eyes,
To tarry for a while and list to him.
While he——

SECOND COURTIER.

         Behold ! she kneels before the king,
As rainbow smiling bends unto the earth.
Darker than storm-cloud grows the ireful
   queen
As she perceives King Herod's fierce applause,
And notes the intoxicated look with which .
He gazes on her child.—List ! lo, he speaks !

. HEROD.

Well done, our peerless one, our conqueror,
Incomparable queen of beauty, grace,
And love.   Ask what thou wilt and it is
   thine,

Test now our bounty, even to the half
Of this our fair domain, and it is thine.
We swear it by the ever-living gods.

GARDEN OF THE PALACE.

———

SEXTUS *and* ANTONIUS.

SEXTUS.

That is her chamber, where the climbing
  vines
Up to the windows mount like lovers bold,
And carry clustering flowers in their hands,
And whisper words, sweet words with fragrant
  breath
In through the casement; but 'tis void and dark,
As is my life when she is out of sight;
That is her chamber, if the lying rogue
To whom I paid a mina for his news,
Did not impose on me—but sit we here
While I await impatient her return,
And when I see her chamber in a glow

With her bright presence thou shalt then depart.

ANTONIUS.

She loves thee still?—thou hast unshaken
faith?

SEXTUS.

Faith! yes, in her forever, faith! why man,
I tell thee faith is weak, is air, is naught
Compared with that great certainty I feel
That she is changeless as the changeless truth.
Why, she herself's the very truth of love.
I could as soon blaspheme the gods as doubt
Her constancy; I know no difference
'Twixt such a doubt and never-dying death.

ANTONIUS.

No absence, then, like dreary, beating storm,
Or dragging fogs, thick chargèd with decay,
Hath sunderèd, nor with corrosive tooth
Hath eaten love-chains thou hast riveted
On her caprices and inconstancy!

5

SEXTUS.

Such absence hath no rust can eat love's gold,
Nor can it break such chains as those which
    bind
My love to me, but only show their strength ;
Yes, it is very long since her sweet eyes
Told me how much she loved, her gentle voice
Gave back the echo, and her heart applauded.
My heart stood still to listen ; then it sang
A pæan, wild with joy, and sent in haste
Hot messengers through every burning vein,
And o'er each trembling nerve to every part,
Rushing with shouts, and calling loud " She
    loves."

ANTONIUS.

Thou talk'st like lovers,—lovers talk like fools.
That must have been a fearful day for thee ;
Thy heart was a volcano belching fire,
And those hot messengers were lava streams.
'Tis wonderful how thou could'st have escaped

A general conflagration—when was this?

SEXTUS.

'Twas at December's solstice—

ANTONIUS.

Fortunate

For thee, the weather was so cold.

SEXTUS.

Since then

Through the long winter of absence have I
    seen

Nor heard aught of her—but I come with
    Spring—

The laughing Spring which now hath just been
    born,

Whose great god-mother Nature at its birth

Spreads o'er recumbent Earth parturient

A drapery of varied, festive green,

Embroidered with beauty blossoming

In every form, in every color rich ;

The whole perfumed with rarest odors fresh

From fields Olympian, distilled in dews,
And scattered by the smiling morning hours;
Calls to rejoicing through her wide domains,
With voice that, thunder-like, reverberates;
And bids her seneschals with splendors meet
Build tall triumphal arches to the skies,
Brilliant with stones of every primal hue,
In semicircles bending vast and grand
Before each cloudy castle in the heights
Ethereal; from pillared forest halls,
And lofty mountain bastions imminent
Hang out her leafy banners blossom-starred;
In every vale and each responsive grove
Collect orchestral hosts, inspired choirs
To fill the vault with anthems jubilant,
While echoes, rushing on from every side,
Dance in mid-air; and from empyreal hills
Falls, like the mingling songs of singing birds,
The sound of bells from shining astral towers.
So I, with joy's harmonious confusion,

By every sign and sound of gladness mingled,
While Nature holds this vernal festival,
Would celebrate my joy-inspiring Spring,
The end of absence, and would find my cure
From sickness of impatience in its presence.
I seek my love, and from her lips will hear
Words, that for me, fill the great universe
With all the music of a thousand springs,
Commingled in one anthem, sweeter tones
Than harp of muse or syren ere gave forth,
Which float on every zephyr to mine ears;
"I love thee ! how I love thee, my beloved !"

ANTONIUS.

May'st thou be cured ! for thou indeed art sick.
Safely delivered of this gale of words,
A hot simoom to any man of sense,
I'll presently administer to thee
A cooling draught.

SEXTUS.

There is no need, I'm chilled,

5*

E'en to the marrow, by thine atmosphere,
Thou art so cold.

ANTONIUS.

'Tis of thy dear I'll speak.

If she seem constant, seemeth still to love,
Some mighty hinderance doth intervene
Between the purpose of her obstinate will
And its accomplishment. Call back thy wits!
Safely concealed beneath that Cupid's locks,
Or in his quiver cased and hidden there,
Behold Perversity, who driveth Love
To conflicts obstinate: and his hot zeal
The unobservant crowd will still declare
To be but proofs of Love's great constancy,
Love's burning, deathless ardor; Love the
    while
Drooping with weariness, ready to die,
Yea, dropping lifeless at the very goal.

SEXTUS.

If my dear seem still constant! If she seem!

Thou talkest emptiness; she doth not seem:
There is no seeming in a soul so pure.
She is Love's Angel!

ANTONIUS.

Nay, if thou dost think
Her subject only to that blind god's will,
If thou dost think this pertinacity,
Endurance resolute of all the pains,
The pangs, the miseries, of so-called love—
Which, from its sufferings, is passion called—
But manifest affection's constancy,
Why out upon thee for a maudlin fool!
And yet thou'rt wise—would that I too could
    dream!
I'd catch bliss blinded!   Yes, I envy thee,
And can forgive thy folly.   May the gods
Preserve it to thee!   Folly 'tis most sweet,
For a most sweetly foolish thing, a woman.
Only be fool enough never to see
What reason drags before thy averted eyes;

Only be fool enough never to hear
What reason whispers loudly in thine ears,
Conclusions damning from most damnèd facts;
Only be fool enough never to feel
The lash of jealousy whi-h reason plies,
And thou may'st count thyself the most blest
  fool
That ever aired his folly on the back
Of that sweet butterfly, a woman's love.
Yet mind thy folly do not get unhorsed,
And break its neck, and reason take its place.
Trust in Love's constancy, and still believe
That thy love's charms are consecrate to thee;
I will not waken thee from such a dream.

SEXTUS.

Thou canst not waken me; I do not sleep.
Nor rouse me from my dreams; I do not
  dream.
Thou didst conjecture well, I'll frankly own it;
Yet thy poor reas'ning is as jester's wit,

A random shaft.   Laughing philosopher
Thou wert well named; for though thou dost
   not smile,
But art as grave as images on tombs,
Thou makest others laugh, and thus in them
Thou dost thy sourness unto sweetness turn.
Yes, we are separate, my love and I
By highest wall of adamantine hate,
Upon whose dark and frowning battlements
Suspicion's sentinels keep their sharp watch.

ANTONIUS.

And thou wilt wait long time, ere they shall
   sleep.

SEXTUS.

Her mother does not deign to look on me,
Save with disdain and fierce lip-curling scorn.

ANTONIUS.

She gives thy merits steeped in vinegar,
To cool her daughter's fever; stay her not,
I am no doctor, if she do succeed.

Thou art a handsome youth ; faith, I believe
That she would hate thee less, if thou didst
    woo
Herself, and not her child.

SEXTUS.

                Something's in me,
Which turneth her ambition into hate,
When it but looketh on me.

ANTONIUS.

                  Were I judge,
From the loud baying of thy most fair parts,
I'd say they've roused that fierce game jeal-
    ousy.

SEXTUS.

Nay, stick to thine own trade, philosophy !
Thou art no sportsman, and thine ear is bad,
Follow but thus the dogs, and thou'lt be lost
In some vile thicket.

ANTONIUS.

              There's an alchemy

Which changeth tender impulse into scorn,
The common people call it poverty.

SEXTUS.

Oh! that I have infusèd in my blood,
And by inheritance made doubly mine;
Father and mother both left it to me,
Not in their wills, but with their testaments.

ANTONIUS.

Grandmother Nature did adopt thee then,
And went nigh spoiling thee with her fair
 gifts
And rich allowance of all virtues rare,
Which thou dost like a cunning miser keep,
And thou do'st well; thou wouldst have more
 applause
If thou didst waste them more.

SEXTUS.

Perhaps, from fools,
Not friends, and such applause would make
 me deaf!

ANTONIUS.

Loudest applause doth mostly come from
  fools !
There was a time when virtues were a dower
Greater than kingdoms; but that time is dead.
Strong though it was, it still began to die
When the soft silkworm luxury 'gan gnaw
Upon its vitals,. spin a gauzy web,
Stronger than iron fetters on its limbs,
And poison with its breath heaven's pure air.

SEXTUS.

If I have virtues they are not mine own;
I may not spend them lightly if I would.
I got my virtues from my ancestors;
My fathers were of that old Roman stock,
That lovèd liberty, that sterner sort
That would not kiss the dust; that nobler
  sort
That could not be enslaved; they lovèd
  Rome:

They loved not Cæsars ; and when Cæsar
    sought
Rome to become, and when Rome Cæsar was,
Then Rome for them a ravished mother was,
Cæsar the ravisher.

ANTONIUS.

    Frankly thou speakest.
These walls may have no ears, but I've a
    tongue.

SEXTUS.

A soldier thou, my comrade; 'tis enough.
This mother's honor quick to vindicate,
My father's father thought it not too dear,
To give all he possessed, and add his life.
It was in vain, and that same Roman name
Thou now may'st read stuck high upon a pole,
Branded conspirator, and left to rot
By that vindictive hangman tyranny.
My father, still a youth, withdrew himself
Into a valley far removed from Rome,

6

Or that which had been Rome, and lived
    alone
With the young Roman girl who called him
    spouse,   .
Who was the only one could call a smile
To his stern features, place a bow of light
On the dark storm-cloud hanging o'er his brow
Ready to give forth thunders.

ANTONIUS.

               Mournèd he?

SEXTUS.

He was too proud to mourn; he held the pride,
Nobility and lofty dignity,
The stern contempt for creeping sycophants,
The mighty scorn for fawning flatterers,
And hatred of imperial tyranny
In him concentrate of an entire race
Of Roman freemen; so have I been told.

ANTONIUS.

Could'st thou not for thyself opinion form?

SEXTUS.

I never saw him; ere I lived he died.

With life to me my mother gave her own.

I knew not whence I came;—I never knew

Mother, nor father, nor the love of kin.

Like the first man I all uncared for grew,

And felt alone like him; for my poor nurse,

Who thought to do me good by rearing me,

Died too, and left me ere I was a youth.

Then I heard tell of great Germanicus,

And then I went with him unto the wars;

And when his godlike eye rested on me

I thought myself like Mars armipotent.

Foes melted at my glance; the battle o'er,

I slunk into myself, went to my tent,

And wondered who I was and what I was,

Wondered why honors could not come with
    youth,

But wait instead to shiver in the snows

Upon the brow of age, and barren die;

Wondered why the rank vine of life in spring
Could not yield grapes and give its luscious
    wine
To cool Spring's fevered thirst; I cried, give
    now
The goblet brimming with concentrate life,
And from its inspiration let me breathe
Thoughts all in flames, or flames in act concrete,
To dazzle the astonished world and draw
The plaudits of all men, that I may be
Placed in their hearts and live no more alone.
Let me flash out and warm the frozen world
With my great, glowing brightness, then con-
    tent
I'll be a blasted crater evermore!
'Twas the delirium of loneliness
O'ermastering my boy's wisdom; I'd not
    learned
That greatness is the loneliest of things.
I wondered if I ever could be great

And win the love of great Germanicus.

He was my god, and often would his eye

Be on me when I felt but saw it not,

Until, one day, with strangely tender words

Embracing me, my valor he extolled,

And in his voice there was a sound of tears,

As in the west wind cometh sound of rain.

He bade me to his tent, and there I dwelt,

And thus I was with him until he died.

ANTONIUS.

Had I such honor I had asked no more

But to have died with him.

SEXTUS.

Could that have been

I had not outlived Rome, I had not felt

The bitterest bitterness of bitter grief.

The greatest he, the best, last Roman was.

In him died Rome for me, and I thenceforth,

No more a Roman, evermore a man,

All countries were my country, every land

6*

My home, the world my dreary dwelling-place.

So that nor country, home, nor dwelling-place,

Nor aught but mine own solitude had I.

ANTONIUS.

That love of country is but egotism

Disguised by virtue's vestures and the name

By one form borne of Protean selfishness.   .

SEXTUS.

I found the earth was very much alike

Where'er I went; ere yet rapacious man

Had ravished Nature of her virgin charms.

I saw but valley, mountain, hill and dale,

Meadow and forest, flowers and singing birds,

Rivers and lakes, seas fawning on the lands,

And islands sea-borne floating noiselessly.

ANTONIUS.

Thou seest; man loves himself and his own
     works,

And love of country calls this—O, for shame!

Party of patriot virtues claims the whole,

And Faction calls its spirit patriotism,
And so it is with its disguise torn off.—
But I'll not hinder thee—I like thy tale.

SEXTUS.

Thou knowest how he died, Germanicus.
With all the ardor of a passionate soul
I vowed eternal vengeance on his foes
Who dared usurp the office of the fates,
And hasten him to Hades in his bloom.
I joined the northern hordes that I might fight
Not against Rome but 'gainst her enemies,
His murderers most foul, most treacherous.
Thus taken captive while I sought to die,
Loaded with chains, along the Appian Way
I marched, a traitor branded, to my fate.
Music's wild bursts sprang quivering in the air
Like jets from golden founts; applauding
    shouts
Struck the swift winds and made the breezes
    reel,

While conquerors' wreaths like fluttering flocks
    of birds
Light on the car triumphal from each side.
A Roman vesture marked me as I passed,
A special object for the frenzied hate
Of throngs unfeeling hurling there their jeers
Like stones and firebrands on the fettered foe.
But as these injuries rained upon mine ears
I felt my stature grow, my heart expand;
I felt a power of virtue in my breast
That made me like a god, and then I smiled.
I seemed to fill all space, and with contempt
Looked down on human malice, scorn and rage,
In soul invulnerable, fearing naught
That human hate could do; thus I passed on.
That night in Cæsar's palace mocking mirth
To Revelry insensate gave a feast,
And mad Intoxication with a torch
Played Hymen's part and joined th' unholy
    two;

While Wantonness attended on the twain,
And lustful License sat as groomsman there ;
And they essayed to ornament the feast
With beauteous half-draped forms, with lan-
  guid eyes,
With mazy motions of lascivious grace,
And with seductive strains of music soft.
By sacrilegious hands sweet Modesty,
Was forced, deep blushing, from her sacred
  shrine,
Her veil torn off, her beauties all exposed,
While on her glared gloating Concupiscence ;
And Chastity compelled to be a guest,
Closed her pure eyes and clasped her pleading
  hands,
In vain entreaty to be sent away.
The morrow came ; the amphitheatre
Like a huge crater hissed and shrieked and
  moaned,
Surging and heaving with the fiery life,

Which mounted up, up to the very top,

Like climbing flames that seethe and writhe
and rage;

And at the bottom Death, with muttered
growls,

Anon terrific roars and horrid cries,

In every cavern, in a hundred forms,

Lying in wait, glared out with blood-shot eyes

From sunken sockets deep, and gnashed its
teeth,

Which thundered with the crash; while the
hot sand,

Like molten lava, lay instinct with death.

I stepped on the arena, stood alone.

In all that blazing life there was no torch,

No tongue of flame had kindled in my life

Affection's glow, nor lit the cheering light

Of gentle friendliness, love's sympathy.

I stood alone. I felt as if all Rome

With all her generations gazed at me.

And by me seemed to stand those giant
    shades :
He who could bear to be death's instrument
On his own offspring, for a broken law,
And by his duty braced, and his proud soul
Wavered e'en less than death ; he who could
    hold
His hand all sensible in jaws of fire,
Till it was eaten off by stinging teeth,
And from the ordeal shrink less than the
    flame;
He who of his own body made a tower,
And of his mighty sword a battery reared,
And of his trusty shield a rampart high—
All to give check to enemies of Rome,
Till father Tiber, on his brawny back,
Should bear the bridge away, which, treacher-
    ously,
Astride his shoulders stood to make a way
For fierce hostility and ravening war,

Then who, ere th' angry foe could intervene,
In heavy armor swam the river home;
The mighty three, who, on their brazen shields,
Their lives did proffer, at the bid of Rome,
To the great three of Alba, should these have
Appreciation that outvalued those
In valor's keen discernment; he who plunged
With his good steed into the black abyss;
And those, Cornelia's jewels, stol'n from her,
Torn from their caskets, but not lost to Rome,
By an insensate mob; with those brave souls
Who in the Senate, on the ides of March,
Approved their mothers faithful to their lords.
Thus, then, I stood, and fear slunk shamed
    away,
And hid itself from me. I did not try
To show I felt no terror, stand erect,
Folding my arms and bracing out my feet,
And putting on the many flimsy tricks
Which the ass cowardice, when in a fright,

So oft mistaketh for a lion's skin ;

I stood as I would stand to talk with thee—

ANTONIUS.

Would I'd been there to have applauded thee.

SEXTUS.

And waiting patiently looked at the beasts,

That lashed their sides, and gnawed the iron
bars,

And gloated on me from their hideous dens.

And then I gazed above me at the crowd,

And calmly followed with mine eye its waves,

Till in th' imperial gallery a form

That was not of the earth, nor sea, nor air,

But seemed all of my dreams to be compound ;

A form of such surprising loveliness,

It were as if the earth and sea and air

To make it up had given lavishly

Their qualities of loveliness most rare,

From their most secret treasure-houses brought;

A form that in its face compacted held

7

More winning beauties than e'er goddess wore,

Pure woman's beauties, richest womanhood,

The gentle tenderness, and tender love,

The loving sympathy, strong fortitude,

Weak strength and weakness strong; that
    modesty

Which, while repelling most, doth most invite.

A form of all the fairest, woman's form ;

A form that mastered me, made me forget

Life, death, past, future, pleasure, pain, joy,
    grief,

The while its eyes looked downward into mine,

Until I felt them meet mine midway down,

And in their greeting kiss, all sense was lost.

For in that moment's meeting of our eyes

All objects sensible seemed to dissolve,

And like a vision pass to nothingness ;

While the interior being conscious grew

Into existence limitless of joy.

This for a moment; then, as if ashamed,

Her eyes withdrew themselves and swiftly hid
Behind her lids, like suns behind soft clouds,
While all her face was lighted with a blush,
Like that which on the face of Hesperus
Is called at twilight by warm Night's first kiss.
A moment more, and she was on her knees,
All the wild impulse of a generous soul,
In the pure bosom of a gentle girl,
O'ermastering maiden shame and timidnoss,
Before Tiberius—"His life! His life!"
'Twas all I heard, 'twas all I saw—enough!
I felt the strength of all the Titans swell
The knotty sinews of my naked arm;
I could have rent e'en Death himself in twain.
And now I grapple him, for I am knit
In deadly conflict with the king of beasts.
Deep suffocating silence, breath of Death,
Mounts from the contest and benumbs the
 throng
For one dread instant; then through all the air

From that piled cloud of faces there break
    forth
Reverberating thunders, peal on peal;
And now they roll away, and seem to die
In labyrinthine caverns of mine ear,
Which grow interminable, as I fall
Insensible, a conqueror on the sand,
Ere the swift messengers of Cæsar's will
Can bear me forth to life and liberty.
From such beginning grew apace our love,
Nurtured from time to time by stolen words,
And richly watered with the maiden's tears,
Refreshed by sigh-heaved breezes, made more
    strong,
And rooted firmly by rough storms of spite.
For ere this love-tree brought forth other fruit
Than tear-drops, heart-aches, long drawn
    breaths, sweet dreams,
Sad wakings, lonely watchfulness and fasts,
And leaves verse-covered, ending all in rhymes,

A thoughtless, tell-tale youth, Ingenuousness,
Though free from malice, did us mighty
harm,
For he betrayed us to Herodias,
As she her daughter with sharp questions
plied.

ANTONIUS.

Then thou wast sent away?

SEXTUS.

Yes, I was sent,
By Cæsar's order, to the army straight,
Where, by my valor, I attained the rank
That brought me near to thee, made all forget
That virtue which they called my treachery,
And made me hope that with its glowing
breath
Fame would consume the animosity,
Or thaw the obdurate purpose, strong and cold,
With which the mother wards me from her
child.

7*

ANTONIUS.

Thou giv'st thy faith too easily, for hope
Is a false prophet, as from this thou'lt see ;
He never prophesieth aught but good.

SEXTUS.

I know him false, I need not arguments.

ANTONIUS.

Why, then how hast thou faith in thy love's
　　love ?
While this enclosing barrier remains,
That caged elf, that cross Perversity,
Like cur in leash, will struggle to be free :
Let slip the dog, and thou shalt straightway see
Desire to stay hath fettered liberty.

SEXTUS.

Nay, now, a truce ; I'll hear thee rail no more.
If thou hast ever loved, how couldst thou ask,
"She loves thee still ? thou hast unshaken
　　faith ?"
I tell thee faith is love and love is faith !

Thou ne'er hast loved or thou would'st ne'er
    have asked

If constant lover have a constant faith.

ANTONIUS.

Yes, I have loved—more than a paragon;

As fair as heaven, as pure as heavenly dew,

As beautiful as morn, as soft as eve,

Modest as silent, thickest veilèd night,

But warm in love as a midsummer's day.

She trusted me, she loved me as her god,

She thought that I would do no wrong, nor
    could;

She gave me blushing lips that did not blush

So much as her soft cheeks; she gave her arms

To twine about my neck, like vines in bloom,

While rose-tipped fingers from her lily hands,

Like pendant fuschia blossoms trembling hung,

She gave her eager, palpitating heart,

That I might feel it nestle to mine own,

And from the twilight heaven in her eye

Shed sweetest dews ecstatic on my soul.
She did so trust me, she did so desire
To make me happy, sacrifice herself
To prove the rich perfection of her love,
In its great fulness casting out all fear,
To give me something more than all she was,
And all she had, and all she ever hoped,—
Had I been offered for that sweet girl's love
Th' eternal empire of a rotund world,
I would have spurned the bribe into the wastes
Of chaos wild and undiscovered space,
To perish vilely there.

SEXTUS.

Now thou dost rave,
As raves a bacchanal insane with drink.
'Twas passion, 'twas not love.

ANTONIUS.

I tell thee, man,
She was my world; my sunlight her regard,
My blushing morn and eve her tender cheeks,

My heaven her eyes, my midnight her soft hair,
My dew the tenderness in her deep eyes,
My clouds her sadness, and my storms her
   tears,
Her lips the billows of my sea of bliss,
Her teeth the reefs on which those billows
   broke,
Her breath my air, my singing winds her
   words,
My two rose-gardens her two rounded breasts,
My vale of Tempe, vale of sweet repose,
The vale between those fragrant garden
   mounds,
Lying in softest shade; my dwelling-place,
My home, my citadel, her loving heart.

SEXTUS.

And thou wast happy? She deserved thy
   love?

ANTONIUS.

Yes, she deserved it, as all women do.

And I was happy as all men who love.
I was as full of lying faith as thou,
And when we parted, 'mid her sighs she
    sobbed
That she could ne'er forget—they all say that,
As they "mamma" say, ere they go alone—
Another ne'er could love, not e'en a friend
Should share her thoughts, by entering dese-
    crate
The temple consecrate to me alone,
Her heart, where her affections waiting stood
To sacrifice to me; her arms she flung,
Her lovely, loving arms about my neck,
And strained me to her bosom, as the earth
In silence hugs the ocean to her breast,
While flowing tears, two sighing cascades, fell
Adown the flowery heights of her fair cheeks.
I wept, less for mine own than for her grief,
And my great tears rained down upon her

And lay a coronal of crystal drops—
Fresh manhood's purest tears on purest brow—
I would that I could then and there have died,
That she had strangled me in that embrace,
Through very ecstasy of passionate grief.
Thus would her love have ope'd for me the gates,
And led me to Elysium doubting naught ;
Pillowed upon her breast, I then had said
That lingering good-night, that last good-night,
And my departing shade would have returned
To say once more good-night !

SEXTUS.

Alas ! poor friend !
Thy selfishness is but too natural ;
'Tis so much sweeter to be mourned than
    mourn !
And so she died ere thy too late return ?

ANTONIUS.

She died ! thou mock'st me, by the gods ! she
    died !

By Hecate, I'll tell thee how she died!
Leaving my human nature there with her,
My loving nature, all my tenderness,
I went with my brave soldiers to the wars.
Her love seemed to have changed me to a god,
Or absence from her to a vengeful fiend;
I sought but to be terrible to foes,
And thus to kindle round my storm-girt brow
Fame's dazzling halo; when I should return
That I might place it on her blushing front,
And say I've conquered this bright crown for
     thee.
I saw above the distant, serried foe
The gleam of armor, as the light of flames,
Rising o'er dimmest night and chaos black.
Then arrows fell like storms of falling stars,
And glancing spears like blazing comets
     rushed,
And flashing swords fell like red meteors.
I revelled in the storm, exultant laughed,

I wrested glory from the grasp of Death,
I forcèd Death to place upon my head
Wreath after wreath with his own grudging
    hands.
I made Death's mighty voice my deeds pro-
    claim,
And when he set on me I drove him back,
Howling with rage, to his infernal caves.
I carved my name on pyramids of slain,
And sent it down to Pluto's dark domain,
Shrieked out in chorus by the flying souls
Of hosts barbarian—and all for her.
And thus I wrought my immortality,
And dyed it royal purple with king's blood,
And put it on me as a kingly robe,
To leave behind me when beneath the earth
I shall at length descend, to be hung up
In th' gallery of Fame, for reverent gaze
Of ages yet to come; thus did I work
For three long years, ere the triumphant host

8

Of Cæsar's legions, from the blood-stained
    snows
Of northern victories, turned their mighty tread
Toward the seven-seated, blood-gilt throne
Of their great mistress, all-controlling Rome.
When turned again toward her I could not
    bide
The spoil-encumbered army's stately march,
But with the winds I hastened on before,
To outrun Rumor in its rapid course,
And be the first to tell my love the tale,
The first to see the ruddy light reflect
Of my great glory in her blushing cheeks
And the deep waters of her beaming eyes,
The first to see her tremble faint for joy,
The first to feel the flutterings of her heart,
The first to feel her short and panting breath,
The first, the only one to see these signs,
The first, the only one to feel these proofs,
The first, the only one to understand

The cause and meaning of these signs and
  proofs—
These signs and proofs, sacred to love and me.
Like valor hastening to the fields of love,
I hastened on, impatient as the storm
By desert heated and by south wind driven;
Horses beneath me melted in my course,
And dew-clad fields grew parched and fiery
  hot.
At last I neared the spot—in nurse's arms
A child, a babe, a twelvemonth old, perchance,
Stretched out its little hands—it was her child!
I took it to my bosom, fondled it,
While my great heart was turning into stone;
The currents of my blood were bound in ice,
Thought was congealed, the world inanimate,
All save that little child which pulled my
  beard,
Smiled in my face its treacherous mother's
  smile;

And then she stood before me in her child,
And then I kissed it in an agony,
And then it smiled again and said "papa."
But suddenly a mist came o'er mine eyes,
And 'twixt the child and me a manly form—
A bearded Roman's form—with mocking smile
And a defiant eye appeared to rise,
And with a look of triumph gazed on me.
Beside myself I dashed away that child,
Her little child, and fled, and fled, and fled.
She died ? If she had died I had been blessed,
For then my grief, roused and allayed at once
By memory of her love, had been a joy—
A joy immensurate, compared with pangs
Which I do suffer now.—But I forget ;
I vowed to curse and laugh, and I do weep !—
But 'tis in jest—think not these tears be real ;
'Tis in this way I humbly do confess
My mother was a woman. I'll forget
That I but half am man, and then this fount

Of salted waters will to flinty rock,

Through sorrow-saving petrifaction, turn.

This inborn weakness, oozing from mine eyes,

Will shortly all be spent, and in my strength

With hate intensest, unalloyed I'll hate

As I have loved!

SEXTUS.

Alas! I pity thee.

ANTONIUS.

Nay, do not pity me; I scorn the thought

Of sympathy for such fool's sufferings.

I would embrace a flame—I have it not,

Nor proof that it was mine, save this fell

smart—

Make me not hate thee by thy sympathy!

SEXTUS.

What was her name?

ANTONIUS.

Her name!—I'll tell it not!

Never again shall that accursed word

8*

Escape its prison-house within these lips!—
And yet—and yet—I think I'll tell it thee—
It cankers in my heart—I'll spit it out,
And cherish it no more—'twas Livia.

SEXTUS.

And thou—where didst thou go?

ANTONIUS.

To the far east,
Where I had never been, where no one knew
    me;.
And there, with a new name and an old heart,
I tried to throw away a blasted life,
Which clings to me in mockery, like a phan-
    tom,
And haunts me always; armies went and came,
But I remained, a spirit of destruction,
Unknown save by my deeds and the new name
I'd chosen; all companionless till thou,
With valor, gentleness, and sympathy,
All unexpressed, didst win me from myself.

The night grows on to its full middle age,

And with its darkness turns my liver black.

If I were not ashamed, and were alone,

This cursèd melancholy I would drown,

Like a blind puppy, in a flood of tears.

I was a fool to be bewitched by thee,

And by my love for thee kept from the feast;

Else merriment had spread a rosy bed,

And I had held oblivion in mine arms.

But now I'll go and sleep upon a thorn,

And to my breast a stinging memory hug.

Yet cursèd memories of all my woes,

Nor weariness of this day's march, nor yet

The allurements of this great and festive city,

Can win from me the burning consciousness

I'm on my way to Rome, nor me content

To tarry on my journey one short night.

I would I dared to tell thee what I hope

And fear to find in Rome;—I dare not do
    it!

Good-night!—I'll mock no more!—and thou
   alone
May'st hotly cherish that fool Fancy's dreams;
Yet, be they e'er so warm they'll naught bring
   forth
But frozen disappointment—now, good-night!

Exit Antonius.

SEXTUS.

Good-night!   Alas! how great a ship was
   wrecked,
And lost its freight on that most fickle sand;
A freight more precious than the East affords,
Though it were robbed from the sun's treasure-
   house.
The winds of Love, that seemed so prosperous,
And followed yielding sails with pressing suit,
By their own favor driving swift the bark,
Caused the great shock, and tore the canvas
   down;
And now the vessel, beaten, drifts about

Till it perchance 'neath leaden skies shall
    sink.

CHORUS, *in the banqueting room.*

Troll the bowl, wreathe the bowl, drain the
    bowl, sing,
Bacchus smiles on us while Herod is king!
Thyrsus with emblems of Venus entwine,
Venus hath colored with red lips the wine.
Troll the bowl, wreathe the bowl, drain the
    bowl cheerily.
Long live King Herod! long live and merrily.

Troll the bowl, wreathe the bowl, drain the
    bowl, sing,
Venus smiles on us while Herod is king!
Tables like those on Olympus are graced,
Bacchus and Venus have met and embraced.
Troll the bowl, wreathe the bowl, drain the
    bowl cheerily.
Long live King Herod! long live and merrily.

SEXTUS.

The revelry runs mad as night walks on,
But o'er my Cyprus gently dawns my day;
My love is in her chamber, and my heart
Leaps up as it would enter with the vines;
And now she at the window seats herself
And gazes on the night—O vision rare!
O bird of Paradise! I'd give a life
Of wildest liberty for one sweet hour
Of sweet imprisonment in that sweet cage
With thee. She loves me still? I'll magic try,
Soft music's magic, and my wand shall be
My old familiar song; but yet I must
One moment more enjoy what seems too rare,
Too glorious itself for aught more real
Than magic's witcheries. What if the strain
Should break the spell and make the vision
     melt
To thinnest air, fading away in night?
Ah! faithless lover! is this then thy faith?

Sings.

Bend from thy window, love,
Listen to my sighing,
While from heated heights above
Zephyrs, slowly flying,
Seek cool vales of earth and lie, beneath the
.   shadows, dying.
. Bend from thy window, love.

Bend from thy window, love,
Listen to my story,
While the smiling spheres above
Veil thee with their glory,
Ere Night's thickly clust'ring tresses shall grow
thin and hoary,
Bend from thy window, love.

Bend from thy window, love,
While my vows I'm paying,
While in milky-ways above

Goddesses are straying,
I to thee, my deity, I to thee am praying,
Bend from thy window, love.

Bend from thy window, love,
Maiden coyness scorning,
Ere dawn, blotting stars above
With the tints of morning,
Call thy lover far away with its bale fire
warning,
Bend from thy window love.

Enter Salome.

SALOME.

Was that some cruel cheat of my wild brain.
Which would torment my heart with mock-
eries?
Was it some echo from the revelry,
Coming to mock me with sweet semblances?
Or did I hear again that signal song,
Which, like a beacon, used, in happier days

To guide me to safe anchorage of love?
Or did my thoughts, by some mysterious power,
Call up its buried image from the tombs
Of silent memory, and bid it walk
Among the hated phantoms of the feast,
Which, leering, haunt me still? Fearful I'll
　search,
While hope and doubt within my breast debate
And anxiously may question of the cause,
Until unsympathizing verity
Shall drive me back with disappointment's
　whips,
Or else, most happy, with encircling arms—

SEXTUS.

Thy lover clasp thee—hush! 'tis I, 'tis I—
And steal a joy from heaven—nay, not a word;
I'll not a breath of this sweet substance lose,
Since, for this blissful moment, all is mine.

SALOME.

Nay—let me look at thee—yes, it is thou.

9

SEXTUS.

Ah! it was I—I think it is not now,
For I so feel my life commix with thine,
That thus, when lost in thee, I no more am.

SALOME.

Nay, still thou art, for thee I feel and hear,
Ah me! and love—I nothing ne'er could love,
Thou therefore something art, that something
    dear
The something I first loved, which something
    was
Thyself.

SEXTUS.

Sweet reasoner! I'm but half myself,
Or something less, and yet I'm something
    more,
For this compounded being, this new life
Is so much greater than that former life,
That this of sweet existence doth devour,
In one swift moment, more than that in years,

All made of days whose hours are centuries.
Sweet love!

SALOME.

Nay—I'll resist—yet could not do it
Did I not know thy gentle strength would win.

SEXTUS.

Sweet life!

SALOME.

Ah me!

SEXTUS.

What! sighs!

SALOME.

Thou talkest not
Tis so much happiness to hear thy voice,
Thy words to me confirmed assurance give
That thou art here—say I am thine.

SEXTUS.

Mine! mine!
I stand upon the pinnacle of bliss,
The very summit of the mount of joy,

O'ertopping heaven's high walls, and look
    within.
I would not lose thy love to be a god
And rule Olympus:—tell me thou'rt not
    changed.

SALOME.

I changed? I did not hear aright—I changed?
Thou art my love—can mists refuse to rise
Toward the sun and wander where they list?
Can tides refuse to leap toward the moon?
When they shall change will my affections
    cease
Toward thyself to rise. Are stars e'er changed
From their bright constancy by wooing winds?
Will they not shine so long as shines the sun?
Thou art my sun; if e'er I lose thy light
I shall be seen no more.

SEXTUS.

        Sweet heart! sweet soul!
That kiss shall tell thee I ne'er had a doubt;

And this shall tell thee that I never will;
And this upon thy sweet, pale forehead placed,
Thy forehead like the soft and crescent moon
Reposing underneath the wings of night,
Shall make thee dream of my sure constancy;
And this upon thy softly trembling lids,
Whose fringing lashes like the shadows lie
On wooded shore of a soft, moon-lit lake,
Shall make thee blind to all my jealousies;
And these on either cheek shall make thee
    know
That Friendship wanders arm in arm with
    Love
Through these sweet gardens, rose and lily
    beds;
And this and this and this upon thy lips
Shall seal my life in thee, so that henceforth
While I am with thee I am with my life,
When separate thou hast my life—I die.——
So silent, love! Yes, rest thy pretty head,

And hide those tender eyes, if so thou wilt,

From jealous stars, upon my constant breast ;

Let not those envious archers shoot their rays

At thy bright, beaming orbs to put them out,

For they, like diamonds shining in the dark,

But still, more soft, have put the stars to shame,

Yet raise them once and give me one full look,

That of't my soul may drink to drunk'ness, give,

I am a very epicure in love,

Without the abstinence which knows to deal

In temperate measure—make me drunk, my
    love,

And speak· one word to let me know thy
    thoughts

Do not play truant, speak one word, my love,

Or I shall coax it from thy bashful lips.

SALOME.

Nay, if in that sweet language thou wilt talk,

Give me a kiss that shall inform my choice,

Resolving all its doubts.   This night, even now,

I danced before the king at his command,
Whereat he promised me with a great oath
That he would give me whatsoe'er I'd ask.
What shall I ask ?   A dazzling coronet,
To bind about my darkly flowing locks,
With burning sapphires clustering on my brow
Like Pleiads hanging on the brow of night ?
A soft and misty robe with brilliants decked,
And silvery purple train like that of morn ?
A veil of golden gauze like that which wraps
Saturnia's rounded form, half hides her charms,
When through the violet curtains of her
    chamber
She comes at evening with her smiling maids,
That I more pleasing thus may seem to thee ?

SEXTUS.

My love, that were a giddy woman's choice,
Not thine, nor mine ; for I so love thee best
Simply enrobed, as sorteth with thy grace,
Thy purity woman's true majesty.

SALOME.

Ah! then I know what thou would'st have me
    ask,
But I'll not ask it.

SEXTUS.

What is it, my fairy?

SALOME.

Thou'dst have me ask the strongest, fleetest
    steeds
That winds of Arab desert e'er begot,
Swift as the coursing, emulating lights
That in ethereal amphitheatres
Contending comets draw, and stellate cars,
And rival planets' flashing chariots.

SEXTUS.

What wouldst thou do with them, sweet ob-
    stinacy?

SALOME.

Why, we could flee away and leave pursuit
To die o'erheated in a bootless chase,

While malice and detraction knaw their checks

In speechless impotence, injustice, pride,

And stern ambition build their flinty walls

Of separation for us fugitives,

Of tenfold thickness, ready 'gainst our coming;

Yet for our coming, bent with captor's chains,

From cloud-embattled towers gaze in vain.

SEXTUS.

And whither should we go? where rest secure?

SALOME.

O we could find some flowery wilderness

In distant, unknown lands, some gentle vale,

Around whose borders in protecting curves,

Above each other, hills and mountains rise,

With softened outlines, like aspiring dreams.

And o'er their ramparts steep, and towers sublime,

Sweet-scented forests spread their flowing
robes

Of varied green, that hang like creeping vines

Upon the bastion crags and turret heights
Of sunny, antiquated palaces.
And on their sides, brooks, hanging, tremb-
　　ling glance,
And waving cascades gleam adown mid-air
Like streamers, which, long since, were shaken
　　out
To the mild breezes on a festal day,
From these same palaces, and left to float
Till lost their colors day by day, and paled
To silvery whiteness, bleached and glittering.

SEXTUS.

Dear tantalizer!　　How should we dwell
　　there?

SALOME.

Our palaces, those mountains and their sides,
The pastures for our flocks, and in the vale
Our tent, our home should be; sweet flower-
　　ing shrubs
Should form its trelised sides, its arched roof

Starred with vine blossoms, covered o'er with
    vines,
And all protected by tall trees that stand
Like thine own strong and bearded veterans,
Or Cæsars, fresh returned from Gallic wars,
In armor green, spears waving in their hands,
Who never sleep, but guard us silently,
Or only speak in whispers when they must.
There could we dwell so happy, nay, so far
Above the ken of common happiness,
That it, for us, would be unhappiness.

SEXTUS.

Ah! sweet tormentor! I did question thee
That I might hear thee say in a new way
That thou still lovest me; half persuaded
    thou
To follow me, yield to my selfishness,
Trust to mine arm for thy security,
And for thy happiness to my true love.
But 'tis not for my selfishness alone;

I plead to thee as well for thine own part.

In soul no longer two, why should there stand

Betwixt us, separate, that iron wall,

Obdurate tyranny unreasoning?

SALOME.

I would, and yet would not, nay, urge me not,

When I cannot with thee I would escape,

But when I can I shrink; I then cannot.

When far from me I long to fly with thee,

But when thou'rt here, ah! then I fear to flee.

We'll trust the power of Love; though he's
    not cunning

Nor wise, he hath a most persistent will,

And he will find for us some remedy.

SEXTUS.

Faith without action doth accomplish naught,

Faith guiding action doth accomplish all.

Though I do love thee more for thy sweet
    faith,

Trust not too much to all-assuming Love.

SALOME.

What! dost thou mock at Love? ah! well, I'll
   let thee,
For 'tis not Love that I do love, but thee.

SEXTUS.

I do not mock at him, I fear him more ;
But I distrust his skilfulness as guide
By wisest ways to accomplishments the wisest.

SALOME.

Thou dost not follow him? alas! I thought
He guided thee to me.

SEXTUS.

            And so he did,
He's a sure guide to thee; he finds thee out,
And followeth thee where'er thou hid'st thy-
   self,
But let him not have reason's torch to bear,
He always puts it out.   I've followed him,
Seeking asylum from malignant ills
That keep from us our perfect happiness.

10

I sought with him a castle magical,
Of which he ever talked, said it was his,
Easy to reach if we would but set out,
Founded on clouds and towering to the skies,
With white-browed battlements and dungeon
  keeps,
And silvery turrets high, and glittering moats
Portcullis crimson, amber-colored gates,
All manned with sleepless guardians golden clad,
As enemies approach prepared to throw
O'er the whole fortress frowning armor black,
And meteors hurl against the hopeless foe.
Serpants of lurid fire that dart and wind
And hiss, and in their writhing folds embrace,
And crush their victim with terrific roar,
Or dry his blood and lap away his breath
With their hot forked tongues and fiery touch.
Within the castle, soft and mellow light
Shed from the myriad precious stones which
  form

The ceilings high, and of dividing walls
Mosaic mirrors make, from which the beams
Reflected glance, and tremble with a sound
Of softest music; couches made of down,
Whiter than plumage which the snow-cloud
  . drops
Swift flying through the air, and softer far
Than wings of hoar-frost melting at the touch.
Nymphs, silver-sandalled, crowned with wav-
  ing locks
Of golden-color soft, and clad in gauze
Carnation tinted, envying not the hue,
Which softer, richer, may be seen beneath
The generous covering, ready stand to bring
Delights of every kind; and smiling sleep,
With gentle train of beauteous dreams, awaits
To bring its balm refreshing to the sense
Wearied with joys, with pleasures overtasked.—
But why doth sudden sadness o'er thy face
Come like a cloud at noon? nay, smile my love.

SALOME.

It were a heaven for me to dwell with thee
In such a place, but ah! I could not go
Against my mother's will; yet I have dreams
Of such dear bliss in fleeing far with thee,
Far from this spot, where e'en the breezes list
To hear us and betray, which I cannot repress.
These dreams have told themselves in spite of
    me;
And I have blushed that they should have
    been known,
Even by thee, and I was self-condemned
That I had thought such disobedience,
And bowed with shame at mine own forward-
    ness.
Such dreams and fancies—are they innocent?

SEXTUS.

Ah! spare thyself, poor child, this self-reproof.
Thou art too tender, yet I love thee more
For that same tenderness; nay, think not on't,

As innocent as thou who'rt innocence—
We found it not, this castle magical,
Trusting no more to ardent love's device,
Whate'er calm reason bids we will attempt.

SALOME.

If reason find a refuge and a way,
Which leadeth not through disobedience,
There will we find the joys which thou hast
    sought.
I'll go before the king and there request
A princedom for thyself, where all thy powers,
The lofty nobleness of thy great soul,
The mighty scope of thy great intellect,
Thy tenderness and kindly purposes,
Thy justice and compassionate intent,
Thy chaste ambition, with its aims sublime,
Thy virtues brave, and virtuous bravery,
Thy pious veneration for the gods ;
All great endowments that do make a man
Pre-eminently great among his kind,

    10*

Shall enter on a stage worthy of them,
And their great dignity; where they shall
move,
And act their parts so much beyond compare,
And show themselves of such a noble stuff
That all the gazing world must needs applaud,
And call them composition nobler far
Than greatest Grecian poet ever sung,
Name thee more noble than the noble throng
Patrician, which, as I too oft have heard,
Doth worship toward my chamber, as the
Jews
Bow down and worship toward their holy
mount.
Then all shall venerate thee as they ought,
And think thee godlike only less than I,
And think me of all women happiest,
Most fortunate, most envied, honored, blessed.
I'll ask a princedom for thee, and the king
For his oath's sake will not deny me aught.

SEXTUS.

O best of all that's best in woman, name
For all that's best in our humanity,
Thy reason creeps not slow by weary steps
But moves like light: ask what thou wilt, my
 love,
And be content, for, be assured, 'tis best.

SALOME.

Ah me!

SEXTUS.

   What is it?

SALOME.

     How I have forgot! ⸳
How I am rendered ingrate by my joy!
Must happiness thus bring forth selfishness?

SEXTUS.

It rather bears injustice toward thyself.
Whence these false accusations?

SALOME.

      There is now

Lying in ward, shut in a prison drear,
A man, a prophet, or philosopher,
Who loves me as his child.

SEXTUS.

Why is he there?

SALOME.

I do not know; those things are not for me.
Yet am I well assured 'tis for no wrong
Which he hath done; he is incapable
Of aught but good, though wise as Socrates.
He hath instructed me in many things,
And I have tried to render less severe
His duress, though he seems to feel it not,
Nor scarce to know that he a prisoner is,
So free is his great soul.

SEXTUS.

What is his name?

SALOME.

John Baptist; 'twas just now, this very eve,
I left him, promising that I would seek

To set him free; yet little did I think

So ready an occasion would be found.

He told me that my search should find success.

Now is the hour; I'll go before the king,

And there demand John Baptist's liberty.

And for our fears and wishes, plans and hopes,

We'll leave them with the gods, distrusting
not

That a good action be allowed to mar

Th'apt accomplishment of our desires,

Since our desires are just.   Thou dost consent

To let escape our perfect happiness

Almost secured, defer maturing hopes,

That we may loose the bonds of innocence,

And set the prisoner free by pious act—

Thine act, of gentleness.

SEXTUS.

Do as thou'st said,

Thy thoughts are God-inspired.

SALOME.

            Wilt thou think
I love thee aught the less if thus I yield
So rare a chance to move all opposition
That keeps us separate and makes us mourn ?

SEXTUS.

O love! O child! O woman! how to find
Names reverend of endearment worthy thee
I know not; I would call thee more than child,
Than woman more, if in the list of names
Of things in heaven, in earth, in upper air,
Or in the realms beneath a name there were
That better named all that I venerate,
All that I love in beings less than gods,
Than that name woman.   Princess of thy sex,
I know thou lov'st me, know that thou art
    mine.
Do as thou say'st; I follow thy pure thoughts,
The dictates of thine instinct generous,
As in the dark I find my way by stars.

CHORUS, *in the banqueting room.*

Wine! wine! beauty and wine!—
Call back the vision of Iris divine,
Passing on drops of a musical shower,
Conjure it, king, with omnipotent power,
Royal wand richly with favors entwine,
Call back the vision of Iris divine—
Wine, wine, beauty and pleasure,
Herod, the godlike, doth give without meas-
ure

Wine! wine! beauty and wine!—
Call back the vision of Venus divine,
Floating on waves of a musical ocean,
Conjure it, king, for thy servants' devotion,
Here to her temple, her altar, her shrine,
Call back the vision of Venus divine—
Wine, wine, beauty and pleasure,
Herod, the godlike, doth give without meas-
ure.

SEXTUS.

Nay, shudder not, they shall not have my
    goddess,
Not e'en in vision shalt thou pass before them.

HERODIAS, *in the palace.*

Salome! say, where art thou, child? Salome!

SALOME.

List, 'tis my mother's voice—nay, I must go.
She seeks me in my chamber—steal away,
But come again, we will together bear
The welcome news of his deliverance
To John the Baptist; ah!—yet, I must go.
But I will soon return to find thee here.

SEXTUS.

Can I not keep thee? Stay, I fear to loose
My hold on thee, lest disappearing thou
Ne'er come again.

SALOME.

      Oh fie! Hearest thou! she calls.
Farewell one moment till I go and come.

SEXTUS.

Farewell, my love; I love to say farewell,
When 'tis but for a moment and thus said.
Farewell, farewell.

SALOME.

Farewell—thou wilt be here?

SEXTUS.

Yes, here, farewell, my breath, my life, farewell.

Exit Salome.

The tide of night, fast rolling from the east,
Is rising to its flood, and on its waves
Stars glide like ships with glittering sails at
sea;
While in yon valley, in that tide's dark depths,
The sighing ghosts of lovers' broken vows
Wander disconsolate, like ocean nymphs
Bereft of lovers, whispering still of love.
I'll go and sigh with them—but no, I'll stay—
This boding silence awes; there is no noise,
Save of the revelry which waxes loud,

11

And grates like dismal croakings on minc ear,

Foretelling horrors; I would rather hear

The direst thunders that e'er yet have rolled

Than that vile raven queen's presaging voice.

I feel as if an omen'd crossed my path

For evil, and I wait to learn some ill—

Hist! what be those strange mutterings in the
    air

As all the furies of hot Tartarus

Were plotting hell-plots over head? I'll draw

And stand prepared; e'en fiends shall fright
    me not.

THE QUEEN'S CHAMBER.

HERODIAS *and* SALOME.

HERODIAS.

Soon as fair Courtesy would let me quit
The courtly company in th' banquet room
I sought thee well;—where hast thou been ?

SALOME.

                                    In th' air ;
Blinded and sickened with the glare of lights
That gloated on me, and the creeping gaze
That fastened, stifling me, upon my heart,
From the blood-heating dance, that caused my
  - veins

In tidal storms to break their thunderous
    waves
Upon the shores resounding of mine ears,
I took refreshment, proffered by the breeze,
In the cool garden walks.

HERODIAS.

                Why tremblest thou ?
Am I an ague, that thou thus dost quake
When I embrace thee ?

SALOME.

                Nay; it is the dance,
Or, 'tis a weariness—I know not what—
That brings me terrors—but I know not
    whence—
Formed formless from a void—I know not
    how ;
But they do shake me.

HERODIAS.

                Thou hast naught to fear.
So thou dost please me with obedience

I'll be thy bulwark; few the dangers be
That would encounter me in seeking thee.

SALOME.

I would obey thee, yea I would do all
That daughter, maiden may—thoul't ask no
    more.
But yet, so please thee, ask me not to dance,
Let me not dance again !

HERODIAS.

             Thou shalt not dance.
Poor fawn ! thou fleest the baying of applause.
Why, thou hast worship had enough this night
To place among the gods a rounded score
Of women, yet thou weepest; dry these tears
If natural, or rather let them flow
Till all be spent; a woman needs no tears
Save those she makes; the natural, briny tears .
Should've been exhausted and their sources
    dried,
And covered o'er with that dry growing moss
    11*

Indifference, whilst thou wert still a babe.

If thou would'st see tears, cause them to be
shed.

Thy tears are timeless now like spring-time rains

In autumn; this is thy true harvest time;

Thy budding beauty springs at once to fruit,

And thou must gather it.   Thy mother dies

Of hunger—let her pluck thy waving grain;

She faints with thirst—from thine o'erflowing
press

Give her to drink, and flood life's ebbing tides;

Unclad she quakes and perishes with cold—·

Let her find warmth beneath thy burdened
vines;

She blanches with impatience, and its fires

Burn hot distress—pass thine untasted cup

From moist, unready lips to hers which scorch;

Give consolation from thy royal wealth—

My child! my child! give me King Herod's
oath—

Let me but say what thou shalt ask of him,
And I am fed, refreshed, clothed, and consoled.

SALOME.

Nay, plead not thou to me: I'll plead to thee,
If I with filial courtesy may dare,
Nor, not obedient, disobedient seem;
For I am straitened, know not how to turn,
Nor can deny, nor yet unperjured give.
I have a promise weighing on my soul,
Which I alone can lift with counterpoise
Of such redemption of his kingly oath
As I may ask the king.

HERODIAS.

　　　　　　Thy mother prays;
Weigh'st thou thy promise 'gainst thy moth-
　　er's prayer?
Come, let me frame thy quest, straightway
　　thou ask,
While wine yet firmly holds its wreathèd vines
Over the eyes of Reason, and ere yet

The weather of the royal mood shall change
From fair to foul. Thy bow of bounty bends
In odor-bearing clouds, from misty wines,
About King Herod's head, and while he drinks
Deep generosity, and feels a god,
Omnipotent to grant or to deny,
He'll grant unquestioning all thou may'st ask.

SALOME.

This once, my mother, let me conquer thee
In pleading.

HERODIAS.

       Nay : thou knowest all my love.
I plead to thee, drive not from thee this love,
Withstanding me. It is a thing alone,
A mother's love, without successor ; dead,
Or fled, 'tis gone, and gone 'tis gone for aye.
There's not in the whole world of human
     loves
That which dare enter in to light the dark
And haunted void, where stands its sepulchre.

Such is my love; although, perchance, I've
   seemed
To leave thee to thyself, abandon thee
To Nature's promptings, let thy qualities
Spring and increase, of their uncultured
   strength ;   .
Yet think not I have loved thee less, nor think
But that I've labored constantly for thee.
What but my love caused thee to learn the art,
Which in itself concentrates every art
By woman found, which flashes more than
   wit,
Which kindles blood more than the burning
   eye,
Half hid in heavy lids, like clouds of smoke ;
Inviteth more than smiles ; thrills more than
   sighs ;
Enchains the reason more than linkèd words,
And lifts the tossing heart more than the
   waves,

Love driven, bounding on melodious song;
Which teacheth modesty to calculate,
And how conceal the least, the most display
The golden treasures of th' Hesperides,
Which she, in scarlet armor, gently guards;
How best to make imagination burn,
And from cold vacancy forge glowing charms;
But chiefly, teacheth timid modesty
How best to hide her blushing self from view;
The art which now hath safely, quickly led
Thy beauty to a bloodless victory,
Worthy an emperor and bloody fields,
The conquest of a king—a royal oath,
In worth a diadem, which thou would'st lose
Through my supineness—

SALOME.

Mother!

HERODIAS.

Peace, my child!
I do not blame thee for't; thou dost not know

The quality of him whom thou would'st save;
Thou knowest not to chain thy heart's impulse
With chilling links of speculation, forged
From reason cold; nor yet hast learned the art
To balance judgment on the silvery point
Of interest; such wisdom comes with years.
Yet may'st thou take it from me in thy
 youth.
'Tis a full hour to midnight: half of that
I would commune with thee to ease the time,
Which else will slowly drag on broken wheels.
Come, let me teach thee life-craft.

SALOME.

        Purely I'd live,
With Justice and my conscience to approve.

HERODIAS.

Talk not of what thou dost not understand.
Justice is shadow, conscience prejudice.
Thou'rt ignorant; I've work for thee to do
And must enlighten thee; and it is time,

For with thine opening buds thou should'st
    begin
T"exhale the power of woman, feel the joys
Of power.

SALOME.

      The power to love and feel beloved
Is all I ask.

HERODIAS.

      The power to curse thyself,
By yielding every power but this and this
Is weakness; thou art strong when thou art,
    loved,
For then thou rulest; weak when thou dost love,
For then thou'rt ruled. Lead for thy purposes
The passions and the appetites, the loves
And hates, the weaknesses and strengths that
    move
And master men; but love them not. Their
    love,
Make it an engine built against themselves.

And batter them ; the weapons which they give

Burn not on thine own hearth to warm thee ;
  send

Them poisoned back.   What's sense of love
  compared

With sense of power, the tyranny of will ?

Then conquer, conquer all that charms may
  win,

A conquest not to be enjoyed but used,

And doubly thus enjoyed in double use.

SALOME.

Naught would I wish to win, all would I give

From him who loves me and to him I love.

I know no use of love save to be shrined.

HERODIAS.

Lift now thy spirit to a hate sublime

And feel the subtlest essence of all joys.

SALOME.

I cannot feel a greater joy than feel

That whom I love doth love me perfectly.

12

HERODIAS.

What are to thee the joys of womanhood
As felt by common women ? Thou should'st be
So mighty in thy strength of intellect,
So cunning of intent, so stern of will,
That thou should'st use thy beauty and thy wits
As if they were another's : let them be
The mercenary hosts of power supreme,
The power of woman's soul cut from the clogs
Of her soft nature, weaknesses of sex
And sentiment and shame and tenderness,
Susceptibility to love and mourn,
By trenchant steel of her self-tempered will.

SALOME.

Mourning's affection convalescent, love
Is grief's forerunner : I would love and mourn.

HERODIAS.

Nay, hear me. Coax to loving strength-proud
    men.
And, to make sure success, draw them apart

And deal with them alone, for they are safe
Surrounded by thy sex, as is the sun
Surrounded by the stars, whose mutual bonds
Hold him in place and from the power of each.
And when the fools are to an ambush drawn
Drive barbèd torments through their writhing
    hearts,
Sharp, racking pains and marrow-burning fires,
And tear by pieces Reason from its throne.
Tempt, tempt, yea tempt always, for men do
    love
Temptation more than that which tempteth
    them.
Let nothing tempt thee save desire to tempt.
And be thou then temptation varièd
To constant novelty ; yet screen thyself
With soft repulses like a coan robe.
Yet so thou be temptation thou must be
Never Fruition ; therefore thou must be
A Proteus in thy power t'escape and change

Thy seeming, with a syren's voice and charms.
Be sparkling wine just mounting o'er the brim,
Receding ever from the eager lips.
Be a ripe fruit just bursting to the taste
And trembling on its stem, yet never fall,
Still bending more and more with luscious
    weight,
Yet never bending to the hungry grasp.
More and more tangible, yet never touched.
Let hope be sharpened by uncertainties,
Possession by anticipation held.
Fetter thy breath, and let it come and go
With limping, labored gait, and bear thy blood
To feed responsive fires in either cheek.
Seem to be all things but that which thou art,
And seem to seem not, all unconscious seem.
Ruling herself, a woman may rule all,
If she of seeming know the perfect use.
The wisest she makes fools, the strongest slaves,
And from the tallest heads lifts off the crown.

She writes the legislator's laws ; unseen
Upon the judgment-seat maketh decrees.
Dealeth death punishments to th'accused un-
  heard,
And sharpens the dull executioner.

SALOME.

I fear I understand thee, yet do not.

HERODIAS.

Thou shalt remember passion is the fire
Promethean that giveth life to love.
And thou shalt light this fire with graces stolen
From heaven.   Remember love's the treasure-
  house
Of kings, passion the fire that breaketh in.
Then kindle it; but see that thou dost do't
Like an incendiary in the dark ;
The torch of glowing posture slyly put,
Its glare half hid by half indifference ;
Or   hooded   flame   of   burning,   down-cast
  looks ;

12*

Or let the spark which 'scapes from trembling
    lids
Be borne to ready tinder by a sigh ;
And let the breast in lightning flashes gleam,
From out its cloudy screen, from time to time,
As 'twere by accident ; and when the flames
Shall wrap the building, faculties stand mute,
Or turn in wild confusion impotent,
Then shalt thou draw its royal treasures out,
Its oaths, its gifts, its powers of life and
    death,
But, best of all, the power of safe revenge.

SALOME.

Revenge is never safe ; I'd flee from it
As from the Hydra. In the wastes of hell
Where from their ashen sources ooze the floods
Which stretch their waveless, slime-envenomed
    length
Through the dread regions of the nether world,
With crawling horrors to their surface filled,

That glare with eyes which wink not, fixed
    and fell;
Where dreadful forests cast a direful shade,
And move and mutter, like the shrouded dead
When they walk forth; where clammy vapors
    brood,
Hatching distempers, while through their dim
    forms
Serpents, with flaming eyes, slow moving,
    trail
Dull lightnings, gloating terrors formless
    writhe,
And lost winds standing voiceless, gasp for
    breath,
There is a cave, mid black, blood-dripping
    cliffs,
And overhanging crags and shelving ledge,
Of tenfold darkness, where no light of day
Can penetrate. There, on the bitter flood,
A horrid monster dwells with serpent form;

At each extremity a hideous head
Utters hot hisses with a fiery breath,
Which lights the cavern with a fetid light;
And on each creeping scale a poisonous spine
Moves restless, and emits its burning juice.
While seeking prey it feeds upon itself,
And grows by feeding; feeding on its prey
It grows a skeleton stinging itself,
Then feeds again, and fattens, on itself.
This monster is Revenge; it bites both ways
And stings with every spine. So I've been
      told.

HERODIAS.

It is a doting nurse's marvellous tale,
To frighten children. Thou, my child, should'st
      be,
No child of common stuff. Thou wilt have
      wrongs.
Woman, with all her power, will have wrongs.
Betrayal, scorn, neglect, indifference,

The mockery of those whom she would mock,

Greater deceit of those she would deceive;

For there be some whom Mercury himself

Teacheth to steal the semblances of fools,

To fool us with; Hyperion's eloquence

And Orpheus' lyre, to charm us from our wiles;

While, in Achilles' armor, they are safe.

And when they've stolen our weapons all away,

They leave our laps with woven net and bars,

Like Hebrew Sampson, on unconscious locks.

SALOME.

I would not mock, nor yet would I deceive,

I'd have no wiles, nor weave a web for flies,

But that which wins shall hold that which I
    wear;

I'd cast no weapons, shear no manly locks,

I'd be Minerva's shield to him I love,

And shelter him with truth; I'd guard his
    breast,

Forever faithful, in my faithful arms.

HERODIAS.

Thine inexperience is spiritless,

And fermentation lacks, like new-made wine;

The action of the world will ripen it,

Till 't shall intoxicate thee, like strong drink.

All women do deceive; all are deceived,

And thou, betraying, yet shalt be betrayed.

The duper duped can never more forgive :

Then let there be for thee in the whole reach

Of nature but one hunger, but one thirst,

One rest, one thought, one hope, one joy—

    Revenge ;

One weariness, one sorrow, one distress,

One agony—the absence of Revenge.

Thou hast not tasted yet the thrilling sweets,

That lie, like honey, in the scarlet cup

Of full-blown vengeance; yet it is a taste

That lifts thee to the gods, and thou becomest

Partaker of their joys, since their chief joy

Is vengeance.

SALOME.

'Tis a fearful thing; the gods,　·

Omniscient, never err; what seems to us,

Seeing but feebly part of the whole act,

As vengeance may be purest justice; I

Would rather leave all vengeance with the gods,

Nor wish to mount to that too dangerous

ht.

HERODIAS.

What! art thou without soul? What! art thou

base?

What! hath my blood to slavish water turned,

To flow in sluggish currents through thy veins?

I'd thought thee formed of metal different,

And tempered with a temper different;

I'd thought thy mounting pride was such,

when struck,

Instead of sparks, like pride of common souls,

'Twould give forth flames, far-reaching, to de-

vour.

'Tis thy young nature which hath not its
　　strength ;
Come, let me strengthen it with this hot kiss,
And breathe a fire into thy chilly heart.
I feel a breadth, a depth of life, as if
No weaknesses of flesh could hedge me in ;
An inspiration and a power of evil,
As I the spirit were of punishment,
The incarnated essence of revenge ;
As if I were t'avenge all my deep wrongs
In one sweet act ; I feel as if my touch
Could change thee from a pure and trusting child
To a stained woman, trusting none ; as if
My word could curse the destinies of worlds ;
As if I should this night engrave my name,
In hissing letters, on the firmament ;
In Hades build a monument to hate,
In mine own image, hating, cursing still.
Come, let me touch thee ; for this night shalt
　　thou

Become a woman; come, and let me bind
A woman's stinging wisdom, cropped from
 griefs,
Upon thy brows, and with this close embrace
Burn all emotion from thy girlish heart,
Save only one, the joy of hate, revenge.

SALOME.

Wherefore should I seek vengeance? whom
 revenge?
No one hath wronged me;—'tis a fearful word,
Revenge! I love it not; pray talk not of it!

HERODIAS.

We love the name of whatsoe'er we love,
We love to talk of whatsoe'er we love,
We love to lose ourselves in that we love:
So do I love that sweetest name revenge,
So love to talk of that sweet thing revenge,
So love to lose myself in sweet revenge.
Thy mother's wrongs, are they not then thine
 own?

13

Come nearer me, come here beneath this light,
That I may see thee blanch and sink away,
In the destroying breath of cloudy words,
While from my burning wastes of memory
I summon up a pestilent simoom.
Come, let me teach thee, for this night I feel
We shall be separated; thou shalt know
Thy mother's soul, and knowing be accursed;
Then shall a vengeance be aroused in thee,
Will not discriminate, nor satiate be.
I think I had the beauty that thou hast;
The summer time of life hath made more full,
And warmed my beauties to a deeper hue,
And changed the opening tenderness of leaves
To firmer texture of the opened leaf,
Brought nascent fruits, but half concealed in
        buds,
To sweet and manifest maturity.
No summer day was e'er so fair, and yet
These verdant valleys and these ripening hills

Conceal volcanic fires of seething hate,

Raging to burst their bounds and overflow.

Why, I was once impulsive, such as thou,

Why, I too loved as fondly once, as thou,

Why, I as madly trusted once, as thou—

Is this the self-same world? Do I still breathe

The self-same atmosphere? Do I still see

The self-same sun and stars ? Do I still hear

The self-same winds and storms? The thunders
   then

Appalled me; now they're music in my ears;

Then storms affrighted ; now they are my joy;

Then o'er my life my spirit rolled in waves,

Joyous and bounding as the summer waves

Chased by a balmy breeze upon a lake ;

Now I am calm and waveless as the Styx,

As cold and motionless as seas of ice,

Save when infernal passions rouse me up,

And mocking smiles, like waves, play o'er my
   face,

And mocking sighs, like breezes, may be heard.

SALOME.

Alas!

HERODIAS.

Call me not from these ruins drear,
The palaces and gardens of my youth,
With thy soft voice; here pleasures dead abide
In ghostly silence; memories here croak
Forebodings sinister; speak not but hear.
I loved thy sire while I was still a child,
Ere yet a sixteenth time the circling orb
In annual voyage had borne me in its arms
Up to the summer solstice, where the sun
Stoppeth in middle course to embrace and
     bless
His planets coming home from wandering.
Thy sire was an Apollo in his prime,
As glorious in beauty as the star
Which leads Aurora up the eastern steeps,
And ordereth the procession of the morn.

Of noblest race was he—a very prince.

His noble soul was nobler than his race.

A prince in strength, a prince in bravery,

In honor, tenderness, and love a king.

There is no manly virtue was not his,

No manly gentleness that was not his.

I know not if I loved him, for I doubt

If love be so inconstant; but there was

A fever in my blood more fierce than love.

In its delirium I saw but him,

In all the noisy world I heard but him,

In all the world of dreams I dreamed but him,

In all the world of thought I thought but him,

And had he never torn himself from me

He still would be my thought, my dream, my
    life;

Thus all my thoughts and dreams, and all my
    life

Would have been pure and noble as himself—

But I forget, and thus forgetting loose

    13*

My hold convulsive on forgetfulness;
So shall remember all my innocencé,
Remember all my wealth, and all I've lost,
Remember how I loved and what I loved,
That I'm thy mother, that thou art his child,
And that great memory will come between
To hinder me from my fore-doomed revenge.
These tears combustive, feeding hot remorse,
I'll dry, deny my womanhood, and pass
With eyes averted the sad sepulchre
Where buried, side by side, together lie
Beyond my sight, twin treasures which I lost,
Those sisters Purity and Happiness.
A twelvemonth we were wedded; thou wert
    born.
Before thy little lips could speak his name
He led his loving veterans to the wars.
His couriers, slain, brought me no messages,
And absence cooled my fever; ere a year
The young king Herod, with his Orphean tongue,

Had drawn my restless thoughts and heart to
   him,
A kingly villain in a god-like form.
I took him to the holiest recess
Of my young life, and gave its secrets up,
And to that self did give mine honor up,
The honor of my lord, to prove my love,
And in my madness, thought that in his care
'Twas fourfold honor ; so he guarded it   ·
As guards a thief the treasures of a king.
He paid my trust with bitter treachery,
He paid my warmest love with coldest scorn,
And for mine honor gave me endless shame.
And when he'd sacked my goodly character,
And pillaged from my temple's treasury,
My woman's jewels, which he flung away
He mocked me, girl, he mocked me, dost thou
   hear ?
He mocked me, mocked me to my face, dost
   hear ?

And flung me from him burdened with a
    pledge
Of love, dishonor, treachery and shame.

SALOME.

Nay, mother, spare me; all thy flashing words
Rush down as thunderbolts upon my soul,
And blast me; spare thy child.

HERODIAS.

               Nay, thou must hear.
Thy father left the army on its march,
Unlooked for, unattended, stood in Rome.
Else had he never seen the accursèd proof
Of more accursèd guilt, prince Herod's child
And mine. He saw and learned the damning
    fact,
But saw not me; then fled Orestes-like.
Men said the furies seemed to drive him on,
And that he sought and bravely found by
    death
A refuge from them in oblivion.

I never saw him more; perchance he died,
For he had loved me better than his life,
Better than all save honor; yet I've heard
From soldiers wandering from our distant
  wars
Of deeds wrought by one hand, always the
  same,
Which could be his alone.

SALOME.

My father lives!
Tell me my father lives!

HERODIAS.

I was the scorn
Of Roman matrons and of Roman men,
And Herod brought it on me, dost thou hear?
I, in a moment's frenzy, seized that child,
As if it were the cause of all my woe,
And strangled it.

SALOME.

O horror! O! alas!

Most speechless horror!

HERODIAS.

                And I had it said
That I had overlaid it in my sleep,
And Herod, this King Herod was the cause.
At length I roused me, as a lioness
Riseth t'avenge her wounds and slaughtered
    whelps,
But stealthily I wrought, nor wrought in vain.
King Herod's brother Philip in my wiles,
By engine and embankment of my siege,
Was woven in and bound with captor's chains.
And thus this goodly castle I obtained,
That from its vantage ground I might assail
King Herod's self.   Yet boots it not to tell
By what enchantment, while yet Philip's wife,
I brought King Herod grovelling to my feet.
And thus I kept him bound; for I had vowed
By all the infernal and supernal gods
To be avenged as ne'er a woman was.

And so I bound him by a fearful oath
To be my husband; Philip in the way,
So much the worse for Philip; he was moved,
That as King Herod's wife without recess
I might occasion watch for my revenge,
And seize it ere it slipped. Nor need was
  there
Of oaths, for to the core I had him fired
With passion, and I held him in the flames
. Till I should be his wife; thus Philip's death
Was not mine act alone—nay, start not, nay,
I told thee thou should'st know thy mother's
  soul
And pale and wither in the baleful light
Of that fell knowledge—I would strangle
  thee
If thou should'st stand 'twixt me and my re-
  venge. •

SALOME.

Let me go hence.

HERODIAS.

Remain and listen—peace.
But when the king would take me for his
    wife
John Baptist, whom alone he greatly fears,
Forbade him, and he wavered; then I vowed
That I would silence John the Baptist; nay,
If he had been a god I would have done't.
Calmly I held the king within my grasp,
Nor ever let his fevered passions rest,
Nor e'er be satiate till I was his queen,
And this bold John the Baptist put in ward.
I hasted not to my revenge, lest haste
Should overrun itself; but thread by thread
I've woven imperceptible my web.
Now the last thread is drawn; let them escape
Who can—and thou—this night King Herod's
    eyes
Were windows for his passions to look through,
And they, too eager, they betrayed themselves.

So thou hast drawn his thoughts away from
   me.
I tell thee he is mine, and he shall be,
To torture with infernal jealousies,
Than which the furies or the gods of hell
Can find no sharper torment ; he is mine
Till I deliver him to furies ; she
Who weakens admiration in his heart,
And loosens thus my vengeful hold on him,
Cannot escape my curse and punishment.
I'll make him hate thee, scorn thee and detest,
I'll make thee feel the gnawings of remorse,
I'll plant fecund regrets in thy young heart,
With bitter bloom and bitterer fruit accursed.
Poison thy springs of life ; and on the king
I'll bring the vengeance of th' eternal gods.   ·
For he shall break his oath, and perjured lie,
Or, me avenging, take John Baptist's life ;
Who, though he seem a man, full well I know
Is from the gods, subject to human power,

14

Subject to woes and human sufferings,
Subject to that most terrible of pains,
The agony of death, and he shall feel it.
If e'er there was aught tenderer in his soul
For me than scorn 'twas pity.   Yet I loved,
I loved him to a frenzy, and I sought
To win his love; his youthful majesty,
His godlike form, his towering loftiness,
His soul that naught could reach, no power bend;
Not all my charms could fire his quiet look;
Not such seductions as have maddened gods.
The more he scorned and chastened me with
     words
The more I loved, the more I bent and prayed,
And when I saw that prayers could naught
     avail,
Nor wealth of charms could bribe, nor tears
     could melt,
That I could not possess him, then I swore
None other should; I hated him.

SALOME.

Alas!

HERODIAS.

And now I will avenge me as a god,

With one sweet blow, and that shall fall on
thee,

On John the Baptist, and upon the king;

Yea, also on myself; yet 'tis a pain

So deep refined in its infernal kind,

To curse thee utterly, mine only child,

That it is sister to the joys of heaven :

Thus I, through thee, will be fourfold avenged.

The hour is come.

SALOME.

There is a holy nymph,

Daughter of Love and Pity, dwelling high

In heaven, fast by the throne and judgment-
seat,

And keeps the book of Justice, who is blind.

The majesty of God envelops her,

And sweet benignity beams from her face;
Of all the forms in heaven hers, the most fair,
Is most approved by all the heavenly host,
Whence Punishment, Revenge, and Hate were
  chased
With all their howling train to Tartarus.
Her angels watch from the high battlements,
To find occasion for her offices;
Her messengers fly home with sighs and tears,
Gathered from penitential groves and keeps,
And prayers that tremble under weights of
  woe.
Amid the perfume-bearing trees, that grow
Behind the throne, a screen from rays too
  bright,
She garners them in her strong treasure-house,
A grotto built of pearl and emerald,
Of amethyst and sapphire, chrysolite,
Chalcedony, sardonyx, topaz, beryl,
And chrysoprasus, jacinth, sardius;

The source whence flow rivers of life, and
    come
The balmy breezes of eternal health :
Her name Forgiveness is.

HERODIAS.

Who taught thee this ?

SALOME.

John Baptist.

HERODIAS.

Ha ! I see rebellion dawn !
The gods do so to me and more also,
If I forgive.   Thou must obey me ! up !
And in the royal presence make this prayer.
Yet stay !—'twere better that thou shouldest
    write,
I will not trust thee now to seek the king ;
Alarm might turn thee from thy charted
    course,
Or, wilful, thou might'st mar my perfect plan ;
Thy timid words might die of terror, ere

14*

They reached the king; I'll find a way and
means

To make thy written prayer acceptable,

As if thou offered'st it on bended knee.

Take now these tablets, write as I shall say:

"To the great king, King Herod, peace and
health!

If it so please thy gracious majesty,

With royal condescension, to discharge

Thy royal oath, hear now thy handmaid's
prayer;

Presently, after midnight, let me have,

Upon a charger, John the Baptist's head."

SALOME.

No!

HERODIAS.

Ha! what ails thee? Hath that Gorgon
name

Turned thee to stone? Bear I Medusa's head

Upon my face, that thus thy stony gaze,

Without intelligence, is fixed on me?

SALOME.

Say thou art not my mother, and content
I will be motherless.

HERODIAS.

Nay, sit thee down!
What! shrink'st thou from me? Wherefore?
    sit thee down
And listen—thou art but a child—'tis fit
Thine inexperience should start aside
At a strange sound, like colts untrained for
    war.

SALOME.

Nay, thou hast made me woman; no more
    child
I still as child am ready to obey
Thy just commands in all things; but in this—
T'imbrue my hands in blood of a just man,
To black my soul with vile ingratitude,
To curse myself with sacrilegious crime,

Never, I swear it ————

HERODIAS.

Perjure not thyself,
Since it is useless; listen yet a while,
Before thou swear'st. Thou lovest Sextus still.
When now I sought thee, camest thou to me
From his embrace;—ay, blush, and thou wert
    fain,
By Herod's oath, this night, to franchise thee
From my displeasure and my hinderance.
Thou still canst do it; write as I have said
And thou may'st wed with Sextus; none shall
    dare
To hinder thee.

SALOME.

I'll not strike hands with shame,
To purchase for myself a life of joy.
Thou knowest how to tempt, knowing the
    worth
Of such a love as Sextus'; O relent!

I am thy daughter.

HERODIAS.

So was she who died
By these most beauteous hands—these tender
    hands—
Which still are strong enough to strangle thee,
And they shall do it, or thou shalt obey;
Quick! make thy choice and write.

SALOME.

No! I can die.
Death is the friend of those who are in pain,
And by the tortured ever standeth near,
To take them from the rack.

HERODIAS.

Ha! think'st thou so?
I'll-undeceive thee; for I'll make Death stand,
With sightless caverns and infernal grin,
And skinny fingers clasped upon thy throat,
To threaten and to torture thee himself,
Without salvation.

SALOME.

Him I fear not.

HERODIAS.

Gods!

But thou art woman, and I'll touch the quick.
Thy lover in the garden waits for thee;
Before, behind, beside him lie in wait
Men who are ordered, at a given sign,
When from the window I shall show this
       light,
To fall upon him, strike him to the heart.
Aha! thou waverest and turnest pale.
What! those bold roses flee thy cheeks, at
       length!
And red rebellion hangs the flag of truce
On thy defiant lips?   .

SALOME.

Spare him! Alas!

HERODIAS.

Finish the writing, sign, and he is safe.

Refuse and, by the immortal gods I swear,
He dies.

SALOME.

Alas!

HERODIAS.

Ay, weep.   Ay, wring thy hands;
When tears thou wring'st from them I will
relent.

SALOME.

I cannot let him die.

HERODIAS.

Haste, haste and write.
This lamp, shown to the angry rising wind,
From that near window, will not out so
quick,
As will his flickering life.

SALOME.

Have pity.

HERODIAS.

Write.

SALOME.

I ask not mercy for myself but him;
Let him escape, I——

HERODIAS.

Write.

SALOME.

O take my life,
Let it appease thy vengeance.

HERODIAS.

Write.

SALOME.

Alas!

HERODIAS.

Three steps will bring me to the window;
write,
Or, in one moment, it will be too late,

SALOME.

Will naught avail me?

HERODIAS.

Write.

SALOME.

The gods forgive,
I know not what to do, nor what I do.

HERODIAS.

Nay, write it plainly.

SALOME.

Ah!

HERODIAS.

What ails thee?

SALOME.

Ah!

HERODIAS.

What seest thou? Turn thy glassy eye—speak;
speak.

SALOME.

As I inscribed his name a cold bright flame
Followed my hand,

HERODIAS.

Thou'rt mad; finish and seal.

15

SALOME.

My arm refuses its accustomed work,
My hand cannot put seal and signature.
There is no sense in it—I cannot see.

HERODIAS.

Then will I guide it, sign and seal for thee.
Ay, sink unconscious; thou canst bend at
length.
I'll leave thee so while I shall use thy strength.

A MOUNTAIN OVERLOOKING JERUSALEM.

ANTONIUS.   AN AGED JEW.

ANTONIUS.

No constancy save of inconstancy,

And of that other thing, that damning thing,

That haunting mocker, mocking memory.

Why, slumber e'en, that used to drudge all
    night

To fit new soles to the worn sandal life,

Hath now become as fickle in her moods

As e'er a woman, widow, wife, or maid,

And will naught do for me but by caprice ;

And then she takes a stitch, it may be two,

To keep together soul and body, patch

Torn expectation, strengthen misery;

Just as a smiling woman darns and knots

Hopes which are breaking, so that she may
  drag

Them more entirely from the tortured heart.

The solemn hour is nigh when eve and morn,

Progenitors of night, do separate.—

Old man, what dost thou here? fearest thou
  not

The coming storm?   The black clouds toss
  and pitch

Like ghostly triremes on an ebon sea;

The struggling winds like drowning monsters
  cry:

The elements of nature seem oppressed

With most disturbèd and unusual state.

AGED JEW.

Languish thy children in chains, thou in the
  arms of the spoiler,

Strangers have gone to thy bed, and the
heathen from far have defiled thee,

Daughters have witnessed thy shame, and thy
sons, they cannot avenge thee,

Rend thy garments and howl, howl for the
shame that is on thee.

Where be thy men trained for war? where be
thy chariots and horses?

Where be thy solemn feasts and the chanting
tribes that go thither?

Where be thy prophets that ruled, and thy
psalmists skilled in sweet music?

Where be thy princes anointed and crowned
by the hands of thy prophets?

Herbage rolling like seas grows red in the
blood of thine armies,

Under its shrouding waves lie buried their
mouldering corpses.

Neigh of thy horses is heard as they look from
the land of the stranger,

15*

Longing again for their vales and the hands
that fed and caressed them.

Roll of thy chariots sounds as they drag, unwill-
ing, against thee,

Driven by hands that are red in the blood of
thy children, to slay thee.

Spread are thy solemn feasts, but eaten are
they by thy foemen.

Chanting tribes come not, but hostile bands
of the gentiles.

Prophets instruct thee no more, but threaten-
ing signs in the heavens;

Prophets shall rule thee no more, but the sons
of unhallowed oppressors.

Psalmists with weeping are mute, and their
hearts with their harps have been broken;

Dimly seated on clouds they shed their tears
on thy towers.

Fettered thy princes, and sore with the servi-
tude heavy upon them;

Sighs and complainings are heard from them
  like the moaning of waters.
Slain is the morning star, yea, planets unknown
  have destroyed him ;
Blood from his severed veins pours streams of
  wrath on thy dwellings.
Lift thy voice for the woes, captivity coming
  upon thee ;
Weep and howl for the days when these shall
  seem to thee blessed.

ANTONIUS.

Thou answerest not ; these portents, these
  strange sounds,
Which seem like voices speaking in the air,
Dost thou not heed them ?

AGED JEW.

I remark them well.
If thou dost fear them go, leave me in peace.
I would unravel their mysterious sense.
I came at even-tide, as is my wont,

To meditate, and mourn our glories dead;
That glorious city is their monument,
And, if I read aright these boding signs,
It soon will be their silent sepulchre.
Mark well her bulwarks, note her gilded
    towers—
City of beauty, joy of the whole earth,
How has thy song to sound of weeping turned!
How desolate! put up thy hands and weep,
Yea, wail and mourn, thou mother desolate.

A VOICE.

Woe! woe!
There be two woes;
Now cometh the first woe!
The dragon standeth on the earth!
His wing o'ershadoweth it, he rules the hour!
A time and time and half a time the second woe,
The woe of woes, the woe devouring all woes
    shall come.
Woe! woe!

PRINCE OF THE POWERS OF AIR.

Rouse up the thunders, bid them mount their
    cars,
And drive till firmest earth's foundation jars,
Uncage the tempests, send them ravening forth,
Unfetter winds from West, South, East and
    North ;
Loose from their shaken prisons raging storms,
Let midnight terrors take their cloudy forms ;
Let airy archers shoot their meteors bright ;
Let flames Tartarean blaze in northern night ;
Let Lightnings take their serpent forms on
    high ;
Let blackest horror cover earth and sky ;
Let each with each contend, and all with all,
Let Chaos reign and Anarchy appall.

ANTONIUS.

The gods preserve us ! What might be that
    voice ?—
The elements are cursed with lunacy.

A VOICE FROM THE FAR HEIGHTS.

Hither, come up ; enter thy rich reward.

AGED JEW.

See ! from the donjon keep to heaven ascend
Horses and chariot of flaming fire !

PRINCE OF THE POWERS OF THE DEPTHS.

Let central seas mount up and lash the pole ;
Let distant oceans on each other roll ;
Let mountain billows rise and smite the shore,
Till earth shall quake with pangs unfelt be-
    fore ;
Let fires infernal lift the solid land,
Shatter its rocky ribs, let naught withstand,
Rush in destructive torrents through the
    wound,
With hissings direful, and with dreadful sound ;
Let tenfold darkness mount from realms of
    night,
Devour the firmamental orbs of light ;
Let all commix, confound, contend with all ;

Let chaos reign and anarchy appall.

A VOICE.

Blood! blood!

A sound of storms! a sound of coming vengeance! sounds of wrath!

The clouds are crimson! mists arise all red
with blood!

The heavy clusters ripe are dropping blood!

The groaning press is sweating blood!

The grapes of wrath are pressed!

The cup o'erflows!

Blood! blood!

AGED JEW.

O Lord, defend us in the day of trouble;

O Lord, have pity in the day of wrath;

Terrors take hold on us; who can withstand,

Who, who can stand against thine awful
might?

In mercy save the remnant which remains;

Destroy not utterly—shall Shiloh come

In vain ?   Shall the Messiah come and find

No welcome ?   None to bend the knee ?   No
   throne ?

Remember all thy promises, O Lord.

Save, save thy chosen, turn their hearts, O
   Lord,

For David's and thy servant Samuel's sake,

For Moses' sake, whom thou did'st ever hear.

ANTONIUS.

The shaking earth permits me not to stand,

Darkness to see, thunders and winds to hear

Speak—say thou livest.

AGED JEW.

                    I am living still.

God hath uttered His voice, the earth hath
   heard it affrighted.

Winds are fleeing away to hide from His terrible presence ;

Mountains are melting to fire, and rocks to
   fiery rivers ;

Stars are withdrawing themselves to hide in
　　the shadows of chaos.

Awful in majesty, justice, the Lord, the God of
　　Sabaoth.

Flasheth the spear in His hand within His
　　pavilion of darkness.

Arrows like falling suns gleam from the canopy
　　darkly about Him.

Lightnings fall from his brows, fiery flames are
　　His sandals.

Rivers are dried by His tread, and oceans escape
　　to their caverns.

Thunders the noise of His footsteps striding
　　'twixt worlds the abysses.

Falling His feet on the orbs, which quake with
　　the might of His going.

Sound of the seas is His voice, and roaring of
　　numberless waters.

Source of the light is His front, and His frown
　　covers nations with darkness.

16

Judgment hath made its decree; the people
are weighed in the balance.

Mercy hath stoppèd her ears, and can no more
be entreated.

Vengeance hath lifted the sword, bright it goes
not to the scabbard.

Cedars of Lebanon come and bow themselves
for embankments.

Trenches about the city! trenches with blood
overflowing!

Sounds of trumpets and cymbals, and of war
the terrible engines!

Neighing of steeds and a shouting! noises of
captains and horsemen!

Groans of trodden on dying! wails of children
and warriors!

Cries of pestilence ravening! cries of famine
devouring!

Voices of prayers unavailing! cries as of women in travail!

Voices of mothers bewailing, blessing the
   wombs that are barren !

Flames ! flames ! flames in the Temple ! defiled is the Holy of Holies !

Voices of silence and death ruling the desolate
   city !

ANTONIUS.

In such a tumult would I were a god !

Fall down, ye heavens, tumble, roar and crash,

Drive earthquakes frightened from their central caves.

Rage, rend, ye cloudy furies, venom spew.

And thou magnificient and black abyss

That yawnest over me, disgorge thy floods,

And blow thy fiery breath ; thou gaping earth

Shut up thy ponderous rock-toothed jaws and
   crunch

Cities and forests, and embowel them

In thy huge carcass ; howl, and storm, and
   rage,

10

Ye elements, in internecine strife;
I would that I could mingle in your broils
As one of ye, and ease my stormy soul.
But I, so strong in weakness, weak in strength,
Can make no greater storm in which to whelm
Mine own; how impotent is man! how small!
These portents bode some evil to the state,
Or to these doggèd and rebellious Jews;
But naught bodes ill to me; I am so ill
In my estate that I a portent am
Unto myself, but can no evil find
Sufficient to relieve me of mine ills.

GARDEN OF THE PALACE.

SEXTUS.

SEXTUS.

Ah me! why comes she not? four solemn
  hours
In livery of hope, have held me racked
On expectation, straining nerve from nerve,
Till all the thews and sinews of my mind
Are well nigh broken, and I shall go mad.
The terrors of this strange terrific night
Have moved me less than what I fear for her.
Why comes she not? the morn 'gins ope her
  eyes,
Awakened by forerunners of the day,
And through the western curtains of her couch
  16*

Looks drowsily ; while wingèd messengers,
With clarion voice, proclaim through all the
    world
Her early rising ; but my love comes not,
And while she come not all is night to me.
Why comes she not ? impatience, work thy will,
And chase anxiety, which more torments.
Strange fears affright me which I fear t'ex-
    press.
If rumor be not all compound of lies
The queen is merciless.   In ignorance
I impotently grope, with none to guide
My hands to pillars of uncertainty,
That I might whelm them with a giant's grasp,
And in their ruins slaughter all the doubts
Which mock and torture me ; why comes she
    not ?

                              Enter Salome.

Ah ! she is there ! ye gods ! how changed ! as
    like

Her former self as blight to blossom.   Love,
What hast thou done?   What hath been done
  to thee?
Where hast thou been? nay, speak to me, my
  life.
What hast thou seen?   Thy hands are cold, thy
  heart
Is almost still.   Have terrors of this night
Chilled thee with horror? froze the founts of life?
Driv'n speech from tongue to thine enchainèd
  eyes,
And held it captive there, forced to proclaim
The one sense, horror, 'horror, horror?   Speak,
Yea, weep, and moan, and sigh and tremble;
  weep,
And let thy tears dissolve the icy bonds
Which bind thy tongue and chain thy strug-
  gling heart.

SALOME.

O Sextus!

SEXTUS.

Why these tears, these sobs and sighs
Which would wreck navies? Weep and ease
thy heart
Of its o'ershadowing clouds; but let some words
Come to the shore unswamped, to let me know
Why thou dost weep, what the disaster, how
To succor thee.

SALOME.

Alas!

SEXTUS.

That tells me naught
But that the weather's rough, and that I knew.
There, there; weep freely resting on my breast,
As, rescued, on the beach the shipwrecked lie
While briny seas flow from them. Tell me, love.

SALOME.

The gods pursue me!

SEXTUS.

Thou art dreaming, child.

SALOME.

Hast thou not seen their bolts this awful
    night?

SEXTUS.

But they were not for thee; the Jewish state
Hath now outlived the patience of the gods,
And they do threaten it.

SALOME.

Nay, it is me
They threaten, and I am undone!   'Tis just.

SEXTUS.

Whence this wild terror driving hence thy
    sense,
Thy reason, trust, affection, yea thyself,
From this sweet palace of thy beauteous flesh,
And dwelling savage there, where thou hast
    been,
Like satyr in a city desolate?

SALOME.

O Sextus, let me weep, nor question me.

I dare not answer thee, for trust hath fled,
And anguish driveth courage from the field.

SEXTUS.

Salome, dost thou then distrust me? say.

SALOME.

I did not say so, Sextus—did I say it?
I know not what I say, I am undone—
To save thee I have lost thee.

SEXTUS.

              Lost me! no!
Thou canst not lose me; thee will I not
    lose.

SALOME.

I am already lost.

SEXTUS.

      ● The storm's obscured
Thy pole star, reason, and thou wanderest.

SALOME.

O Sextus, curse me not; my shattered bark
Is sinking now with woe; not one hour tried

Under my guidance, when the storm came
 down,
Out of a summer sky on summer seas,
And it is wrecked, and driven out so far
On stormy oceans it can ne'er return,
But now must drift alone till I'm ingulfed,
Striving in vain to steer my way to heaven.

SEXTUS.

Salome, cease these mysteries, and speak
In plain, unstudied words, that which thou
 meanest.

SALOME.

Let me withdraw myself, while strength remains,
Nor make me make thee chase me from thy
 breast.
I'd have thee weep for me, and not abhor.

SEXTUS.

Dost thou distrust me when I should be strong,
But trustest me in weakness? Do me not

This wrong to my poor manhood; I could wield
Great Neptune's trident, to make down the waves
At thy command, and drive the hostile winds
Back to their caves, and bar them fettered there.
I'll be thy cure; thy childish brain is crazed!

SALOME.

Yes, I am crazed: think but that I am crazed,
And that my hurried words are but the clouds
From a distempered sea, and let them pass.
This night indeed hath been an awful night,
And fearful things were heard; but fearfulest,
Unseen, unfelt, unheard, except by me,
The mysteries horrible which call me hence.

SEXTUS.

Thou would'st not go from me again?

SALOME.

I must!

SEXTUS.

Whither?

SALOME.

I cannot tell; but I no more
Shall see thee.

SEXTUS.

Oh! thou provest me, to know
How much I love thee.

SALOME.

I would keep thy love.
Therefore I part from thee. I could. e'en
 bear,
If time and purpose could excuse, to lift
A suicidal hand against myself;
But cannot bear this fond desire I feel
To tell thee all should crucify thy love,
And rob me of it. Love me always, Sextus.

SEXTUS.

I will, I will, I will. 'Tis said caprice
Rules woman, yet I know it hath no place
17

In thee, but that thou'rt moved by weighty
    cause;
Then let me see it; I will run it through,
And with a thrust of reason take its life.

SALOME.

Could I but tell thee all I've heard and seen,
Could I but tell thee all that I have done,
 And yet not drive thee shuddering from my side,
I'd do it, weeping tears of gratitude
For such relief.

SEXTUS.

    Naught can drive me from thee.

SALOME.

I've come to say farewell, and my poor heart
Is breaking; tell me not how thou would'st
    guard,
Guide, shelter, aid and love me, or, alas!
I cannot leave thee.

SEXTUS.

    And thou never shalt.

SALOME.

I love thee so.

SEXTUS.

My angel.

SALOME.

Hold me tight.

SEXTUS.

Closer than life.

SALOME.

One moment more.

SEXTUS.

For aye.

SALOME.

Now kiss me on mine eyes, and charm away
That which doth haunt them. Dost thou love
me still?

SEXTUS.

Salome! pity me; what dost thou mean?

SALOME.

And thou wilt love me always?

SEXTUS.

Naught but thee.

SALOME.

Thou wilt remember me when I am gone ?

SEXTUS.

Thou shalt not go ; imprisoned in these arms,

No power shall take thee thence, not e'en thine

own.

SALOME.

I am already gone. That which thou holdest

Is the last shadow of that which I was,

Passing away and mingling into night.

Ah! press me closer, nearer to thy heart ;

Another kiss for friendship, one for love,

Another for forgiveness pardoning all,

And so farewell, O heart, O life, farewell.

SEXTUS.

Salome! I cannot entreat ; behold

My silent anguish, let it plead for me.

What can I say to thee more than I've said,

For when I said I loved thee I said all.

I've wooed thee even so as best I could ;

I've wooed thee as a soldier, told my love

In honest phrase that hit its mark ; unskilled

With many words to weaken love's avow.

My heart is strong enough to suffer strongly.

I would 'twere weak enough to weakly break,

So woo thee brokenly, with broken words

Out of my broken heart, and thus might
    break

Thy too resolvèd purpose, which, too hard,

Should easily be broken. I would say

With such doubt-breaking truth I love thee,
    thou

Could'st doubt not ; I cannot abase myself,

Using great oaths, to swear that I do love ;

Yet, when I tell thee solemnly I love,

It is an oath itself the solemnest,

Pledging mine honor to thine honored trust.

If thou dost doubt me of thyself, 'tis well ;

   17*

I'll doubt myself henceforth, and trust but thee;

And having said this much, with naught to add,

I'll bow to thy decree as 'twere a god's.

But if another have infused in thee

Some loud suspicion, or some whispering doubt,

I pray thee listen rather to the voice

Of thine own justice and thine own pure heart,

For I am conscious of integrity,

Nor may I guess by what disjuncture we

Are to be separated, nor the cause.

SALOME.

It is myself.—O thou wilt break my heart!

I never doubted thee.   I love thee more

Than words a maiden's tongue can find, could
    tell.

I am accursèd—shudder not, nor look

On me with half-averted eyes, nor loose

The pressure of thine arms when thou shalt
    know

All that I have to tell.

SEXTUS.

Speak.   Tell me all.
Nothing can change my love, for I am thine
To watch and guard, to succor and to keep,
To love thee until death.   My word's myself.
I've given thee my word.   If woes assail,
They are for me; if blessings fall, for thee.
Woes turned from thee by me, for me are joys.
Whether with thee, admitted to thy court
Or banished from thy presence, I shall be
At all times blessed by this one consciousness
I'm watching over thee.

SALOME.

O noble soul!
Tis I the exile, banished by mine act
From kingdom, country, paradise, in thee.
I am undone—a murderess accursed,
With all the curses of Orestes cursed.
I've raised my hand against a man of God,
And ta'en away his life.   The gods avenge!

O sacrilege !   O death !   O infamy !

SEXTUS.

Alas ! alas !   I hear thee in a dream.

SALOME.

What could I do ?   To save thee, save thy life,
I asked John Baptist's, thereunto compelled
By mine own mother! and they brought his
  head :—
'Tis there!—it smiles on me !   O blind mine
  eyes !
O horrible ! alas !   O woe is me !

SEXTUS.

Hush! hush! I'm with thee ; there is naught
  to fear.

SALOME.

And now I am accursèd, and must go
To expiate my crime in holy acts
Of charity and self-denial, pains
And fastings penitential which may move
His God to pity.

SEXTUS.

Heart most generous!
Thou doest all for me, bravest all risks,
And I do naught for thee.—Thy woman's
strength
Of generosity and fortitude
Puts all my manhood's virtues to the blush.—
But think what thou would'st do and do it
not.

SALOME.

Among his people is a vestal sect
Founded by one unfortunate, like me,
Unlike me guiltless, Jephthah's doomèd child,
Who gave herself to charitable deeds ;
And many maidens joined themselves to her,
And others unto them, in charity
Seeking atonement, or relief from woes.
Abjuring all that others hold most dear,
They live a benefaction to their race.
Thus will I do, and thus atone my sin.

SEXTUS.

Nay, be not so deceived; thou hast no sin.
Nay, be not so unjust to thee and me.
Who acteth by compulsion acteth not ;
Not his the merit nor demerit ; thought
Is act before the gods who judge us.   Act
Is but the body, thought the acting soul.
I cannot let thee do thyself this wrong.

SALOME.

But I resisted not; nay, yielding turned
Into a murderous sword a harmless style.
Of tablets innocent I made a block,
And thus, a trait'ress, took my master's life.
O horror ! O alas ! O infamy !
Nay, drive me from thee.   I unworthy am
That thou should'st look upon or hear me
    speak.
Thou could'st not with Assassination wed,
Nor could'st hold Sacrilege in thine embrace.
The gods abhor me !   I abhor myself.

All nature shrieks at me and hides its face.
Undone! accursed! O, woe is me! alas!

SEXTUS.

Ah! cease this mourning, love—thou wert
constrained.

SALOME.

O I've heard words this night would blight an
oak,
Cedars of Lebanon clothe with hues of death.
I've learned to pity me that I was born,
And wonder that my blood sprouts not with
crime
Of its own natural action.

SEXTUS.

My poor child!

SALOME.

Nay, send me from thee.   I can never be
That which I was; for, stricken is the flower.
The springs of joyousness, which give the
sap

To youth, are dried, and cankered are my
    roots;
Thou shalt find naught but blights upon me,
    blights.
No verdure decks my branches; pallid leaves
Move lifeless in the breeze, too soon to fall.
Let me be prompt to loose thee from thy vows ;
My vows are dead, for she who made them's
    dead.
I am not she—I know not who I am.
But had I been myself I would have died
Rather than shed the blood of that just man.
Yet thus should I have been thy murderess.
What could I do? how turn? O gods, have
    pity.

SEXTUS.

They will have pity ; calm thyself, my life.
I'll help thee ; we will help each other, love.

SALOME.

Where light shall go, the shade of **infamy**

Shall rest upon my name, historians tell
The history of this sight to blacken me,
And dying I shall live, by all condemned;
Yet when they shall condemn me, as they will,
And shuddering breathe my name, when they
    must speak it,
And use it for a curse, then say for me,
Salome was a woman pressed by fate,
And overcome by fierce disaster; say
She was a woman, not more weak than others,
But that she was o'ercome by fiercer foes;
That calmest waters in her sea of life
Opened a whirlpool, and that she went down
In wilder tumults than Charybdis' whirls,
To deeper depths; she struggled as she could,
And struggling sank.   She was more forced to
    sin
Than sinning; yet was weak, and so was forced;
But, mourning what she's done, could not
    again
18

Do otherwise.   Say she was, like her sex,
Too strong for weakness and too weak for
    strength ;
And, thus excusing her t'injustice, say,
In the great court of human prejudice
She prayed consideration of her woes.

SEXTUS.

O noble heart !   O courage most sublime !
O let me win thee from this cursed belief.

SALOME.

My heart is breaking ; naught can bind it up,
I love thee so I would not have thee suffer ;
And yet didst thou not suffer I should be
In tenfold misery.   Nay, be not sad—
It is the will of God ; we must submit.

SEXTUS.

Salome ! wilt thou surely leave me thus ?
Hast thou preserved me from oblivion
To put me in the flood with Tantalus ?
To make me live, knowing that thou dost live,

But that I ne'er can see thee, speak to thee,
Console thee in thy grief, nor hear thee speak,
Quenching the thirst unquenchable of love
By saying that thou lovest me, giving me
The holy right to kiss away thy tears?
Salome! O Salome! think of this—
How lonely, lifeless, desolate the world!

SALOME.

Sextus, thy words have ta'en from me my will,
And I am feeble as a little child,
Am torn in twain by duty and desire.
I cannot stay with thee, it were the price
Of my great crime; for when she urged me on
The queen consented that I should be thine.

SEXTUS.

Thus from the very gates of Elysium,
For which we've toiled so long, endured so
    much,
Prayed waiting, hoping, longing, weeping, nay,
Ready to take the battlements by storm,

Thou castest me to torments by a word.

SALOME.

I know not how to leave thee ; gods exact
The sacrifice and they will give me strength.
I never loved thee as I love thee now.
I never knew before the depth of joy
To feel thine arms protecting, holding me,
To hear thy voice dispelling all alarm,
And filling me with calmness, making life
One joy concentrated of every joy ;
Yet, ere the sun shake from his glittering locks
The gleaming dust caught from his golden
    pillow,
I must be far beyond the city walls.
When cometh weeping night with dewy tears,
And the sad nightingale mourneth her mate,
Then will I dare to weep for thee and me ;
Nor fear to sin in feeling such regrets
As our first mother felt, when forth she went
From Paradise, as I have heard relate,

Since such regrets are my great punishment.

SEXTUS.

Salome! this is death, long, living death.

SALOME.

Dawn moves aside before the coming day.

I dare not longer tarry, fare thee well.

The gods preserve thee, gods almighty bless,

Comfort and counsel thee, Sextus, my love,

My life, my hope, my future, present, past.

Abhor me not, farewell—farewell—farewell.

18*

THE QUEEN'S CHAMBER.

HERODIAS WITH JOHN BAPTIST'S HEAD.

HERODIAS.

At length I am avenged; drink, drink, my soul,
The sweet conviction, drink till thou be drunk.
The king, smitten of God, before his time,
Eaten, alive, of worms, in torment howls,
Calleth for death that comes not, shall not
    come,
Till all the horrors of the sepulchre,
The crawling, gnawing worms, slow-feeding
    fires
Which open their dull phosphorescent eyes

Only in darkness, putrefaction black,
And stifling mould, which shoots its creeping
    roots
And grows to forests, crushing flesh to dust,
Shall in his life be felt; his body thus,
Not dying but consumed, his soul shall go
Swift to black Hades and Tartarian woe.
Salome, from the world self-banishèd,
Seeketh to find her exile in the world,
And by self-punishment to make amends;
Self-judging, self-accused, and ignorant
That man may pray and pray and still be
    damned,
May practise charity and still be damned,
Inflict self-punishment and still be damned;
Forgetful that, if there be real offence,
Th' offended power alone can name the price
Of full forgiveness—'tis her fantasy,
Led on by virtue—virtue's such a fool!
And thou, sweet head, yea, thou art mine at last.

What! thou canst smile while I do speak to thee?
I thought my voice, like a storm-breeding wind,
Would drive that smile away, and bring a
　　frown
To flash its lightnings from thy brow of heaven.
Thy heart's too stony—that I will not have.
I wonder it could give even these red drops.—
Come they indeed from thee? I'll taste this
　　blood.
Methinks I'd know the taste of thine own blood.
I would have mingled all thy blood with mine,
And sent it forth in such heaven-daring life
That e'en Prometheus in comparison
Should fail in enterprise, and all the Titans
Pigmies and cowards be; could that not be,
I would have given all my blood to thee.
But thou disdainedst me; from these smiling
　　lips
I've heard the only words I ever heard
Since tearful Innocence bid me good-bye,

A weary time ago, could make my blood

Mount from my heart to watch-towers of my

 cheeks,

To see who thus so loudly summoned it.

Thou'st paid the penalty of thy disdain.

Where was thy God? Could He not save thee,

 then?

Is there then naught a woman may not do?

Now will I e'en defy thy God Himself,

And in His temple will I make my bed,

And on His altar will dream dreams of thee,

My sweet: some living semblance of thyself,

With blood that floweth not so cold as thine,

To be my fellow in the holiest place.

What! thou dost frown at last! 'tis thine old

 trick,

When I did meet thee. 'Twill not fright me

 now,

Nor turn me back, nor make me hold my tongue.

Now thou art mine, I can embrace thee even,

And weave my lily fingers in thy hair,
And stroke thy temples, fondle thee, and hate.
Call thyself back to life, and list to me
While here I mock thee, spurn thee, spit on
thee.
Why liest thou there? What! would'st thou
plead to me?
Ah! thou art very pale; where is the health
That blossomed like a garden in thy face,
And brought forth manly beauty? where the
flush
Of indignation or of shame whene'er
I spoke to thee? Come, let me call it back
With words would shame the satyrs in their
dens.
It comes not! what! comes not! Thy virtue
sleeps,
And all thy blushes which have guarded it
Have run away to cool in this flat dish.
I'll with my fingers put them in their place

On thy pale cheeks, yea, even on thy brow,

Or summon them with my all-potent kiss.

Come, let me press thy virtuous, scornful lips—

A VOICE.   .

Go to thy place.

HERODIAS.

.   Oh! horror! life! Oh! death!

A WOOD.

SALOME.

SALOME.

Here will I rest me till my maidens come
To mourn with me.   In such sweet solitude,
Where love and longing to behold create
A presence sensible of the beloved,
I shall, henceforth alone, not be alone.
Yet is this presence to my conscious heart,
As circumambient mist to thirsty souls,
Th' intangible presentment of their wish.
Alas!   I never more may look for showers,
Nor dews, nor springs, nor rivulets nor lakes;
But far before me to the vast and dim,

The infinite of space, a desert drear
Stretches interminable; scorching sands
Return the glare of a more scorching sun,
And sluggish winds, like the hot tainting
    breath
Of fiery monsters, burn and blast my cheek.
I'll go to deeper shade and solitude;
For deepest solitude is solitude
Least deep for me; for I am so dissolved
To unsubstantial being by the void
Of beings substantive and sensible,
That with the unsubstantial forms of love
I may hold converse; my reality
Thus disappearing, they are real to me.
I thus am still with him who's love to me.
Here will I rest while o'er my head the trees,
Hoary with moss, hold out their trembling
    hands,
With voices soft, like holy priests at prayer,
They pray for me; while in the vale the brook

19

In reverence leaves its leaps from stone to
stone,
And solemnly and softly goes on sand.
The birds have ceased their earlier morning
songs,
And listening with bent heads and folded
wings,
They only say amen from time to time.
Prayer dwelleth in this place; the gods are
near.
O God, behold my utter helplessness,
Have pity on my utter worthlessness,
Redeem me from my utter guiltiness,
And purify me with thy righteousness.

JESUS.

Salome!

SALOME.

Sir!

JESUS.

Why weepest thou?

SALOME.

Alas!
I am oppressed with sense of grievous guilt,
Nor can I find relief, nor know I where
To turn for help or comfort; here, condemned,
I seek a way to expiate my crime,
While conscience, restless, will not let me
 rest,
Approves of naught, and will not let me
 choose.

JESUS.

I am the Way.

SALOME.

Sir, who art thou?

JESUS.

The Truth.

SALOME.

What canst thou give to guide me to the way?

JESUS.

The Light.

SALOME.

I'm lost!

JESUS.

I came to save the lost.

SALOME.

Ah ! my offence is registered in heaven.

JESUS.

Atoning blood can wash the record out.

SALOME.

What is the sacrifice?

JESUS.

The Lamb of God.

SALOME.

Where is the Lamb of God?

JESUS.

Behold Him here.

Salome, nor the blood of beasts nor birds,
Nor penitential pains and misery,
Could e'er atone for the offence of man ;
But when he was thus lost, and lay condemned

In the stern prison-house of endless death,
God lovèd so the world He gave His Son,
That whosoever would believe on Him
Should perish not, but have eternal life.

SALOME.

Where is the Son, that I too may believe?

JESUS.

It is the Lamb of God; believest thou?

SALOME.

I would believe; help thou mine unbelief.

JESUS.

The children shall not for the parents die.
Each for himself shall bear iniquity;
And Christ for all who shall come unto
Him.
For whosoever shall believe on me,
Though were he even dead, yet shall he live.

SALOME.

Art thou then He of whom John Baptist
spake?
19*

JESUS.

I am.

SALOME.

Lord God, take all my guilt away.

JESUS.

Thy faith hath saved thee; thou may'st go in
peace.

SALOME.

May I not follow thee?

JESUS.

Thou shalt; but learn

That they best follow me who best fulfil

Their duties to their race as God ordained,

Loving their neighbor even as themselves,

And God with all their heart, and soul, and
mind;

By being true to those whom God hath bound

In clusters with them on the vine of life.

Not in the literal and formal act,

With due observance of religious rites,

And many words professing me as Lord,

Am I best followed.   They who follow me

In spirit and in truth, best follow me ;

And they shall be the favorites of my fold,

And I shall know them though the world do
   not ;

And I will love them. They shall keep my
   words,   .

Which, grafted in them, spring t'eternal life.

Who thus shall follow me shall ne'er taste
   death.

SALOME.

Instruct me, that I thus may follow thee.

GARDEN OF THE PALACE.

———

SEXTUS *and* ANTONIUS.

ANTONIUS.

WHAT! Sextus! what! dost sleep? Arouse thee,
man.

The dawn hath climbed the heavens, and, one
    by one

Plucked the ripe stars; thou should'st ere now
    have filled

Thy garner full of sleep, and harvested

Thy rest. Wilt thou away with me to Rome?

SEXTUS.

To Rome? ay, anywhere; let's go at once.

ANTONIUS.

What ails thee, Sextus? why this pallor strange?

This recklessness of haste? Why hang'st thou
    out

Those signals of distress on either lid?

Why shine those tears like beacons on éach
    cheek?

SEXTUS.

I am a coward—cowards may shed tears.

I have been wounded.

ANTONIUS.

                That is plain enough.

No blood is left in thee; those ruddy lakes

On either side the mountain ridge of thy face,

Which flashed with crimson light beneath thine
    eyes,

Have all run out, and left pale, empty beds,

And there's not light enough in thy dull eyes

To light a maiden's trembling lips to thine.

Say, hast thou watched in vain? Hath she
    not come?

Or hath the storm capsized thy youthful wits?

SEXTUS.

The storm? what storm? Ah! yes, I mind
 me now.
How went the storm abroad? what hast thou
 seen?

ANTONIUS.

More wonders than portended Cæsar's death.
In heaven two stars came down from th' Al-
 mighty throne.
The first was brighter than the brightest
 star;
The second, brighter than the sun at noon,
Followed the first a little way behind.
The first in form a man; the second God.
A wandering planet rose and took the first;
And cast it from its place and put it out.
Then all the planets came together, stood,
And lifted up the second on a cross,
Which spanned the heavens and covered the
 whole earth.

And when the second bowed its head and died,
Deep darkness filled th' entire universe,
And all the stars burned dimly and went out.

SEXTUS.

What might this mean?

ANTONIUS.

I know not; 'tis a sign
Beyond my comprehension; in the womb
Of destiny some era or event
Most marvellous is struggling for its birth.
And there were sounds of voices in the air
Like sounds of oceans teased by wanton winds;
The earth with ague shook and gasped with pain.

SEXTUS.

I heard them; they portend no good to us.

ANTONIUS.

The night was savage, freshly come from chaos;
The wild winds sobbed like wailing goddesses,
Lifted their voices, tore their cloudy hair,
While fires burned pale in the black firmament.

Just now a Jewish soldier of the guard,
Half dead with fear, recounted unto me
The things that he had seen. The donjon
    shook
And quivered with a murmur to its base;
While in the temple of these rebel Jews
The ever-burning fires went out; the graves
Of th' prophets ope'd, and hoary they came
    forth,
And o'er the city stretched their bounden
    hands,
In silence weeping; then in awful state
Of ghostly apparition they moved on,
Like white clouds moving through the mid-
    night air,
Toward the donjon tower, procession weird.
Then from the topmost turrets of the keep
A flame arose and disappeared in heaven.
The ghostly forms once more stretched forth
    their hands

Over the city, turning every way,

And with one voice a simultaneous woe

Pronounced, which wailing, rolling, fading,
    died

In thunder, as they slowly disappeared.

Upon the temple's highest tower stood

A form of fire, and held a blazing sword,

And brandished it in mazy lightning strokes

Over the city; then he disappeared.

Like wailing forests and the ocean's roar,

Sounded afar his flaming chariot wheels.

Sure these are signs enough to shake the nerves

Of older men than thou, and conjure fear

From 'ts coward hiding-place—if thou dost
    fear—

SEXTUS.

I fear?—thou know'st not what thou say'st—I
    fear?

Why yes—I fear myself—I will not boast

My courage; it is gone—I am afraid.

20

Antonius, spare me thy raillery,
And I will tell thee all.

ANTONIUS.

              Tell me, my boy ;
I do divine it now ; but tell it me,
And thou shalt see I have a heart can feel,
As well as hide its tenderest, bitterest part.

SEXTUS.

I ne'er shall see Salome more.

ANTONIUS.

                  Alas!
Thou could'st not profit by experience
Of mine ; I gladly would have saved thee this.
Women are learning always ; they would know
How tasteth the forbidden and unknown.
Therefore are they not constant ; constancy
Content learns not ; who would have knowledge
     reads
In many books ; who holds through life to one
Reads not at all, but thumbs its freshness off,

Like school-boys in their ignorance content;

The index known.the book is put aside.

Thus women read us as a library;

And thus they know our weakness and our
strength

Better than we ourselves. Nay, be a man,

Nor let me see in thee another wreck

Foundered on quicksands of inconstancy.

SEXTUS.

O she is constant as the constant tides

Whose ardor centuries of failures damp not,

But, still as eager as on the first day

When they were driven back from kissing
heaven,

They still leap up with panting, foaming lips,

Up to embrace the sky, like hounds in leash

Held back and dragged away to come again.

O she is constant, but the destinies,

By her too tender conscience, drag her hence

They've taken her away, and now she goes—

Led from me, looking back and mourning still.
Hence, hence with me, and I will tell thee all;
I will recount to thee my misery,
Its cause, its fashion and its hopelessness.
But this thou shalt believe, that she is con-
    stant.

ANTONIUS.

I will, when I believe that fire is cold.
Ice hot, sun night, night noon, an arrant thief
A safe companion for an honest man,
Or honesty is kept in beauteous caskets.
Then will I think that honesty is found
Encased in woman.   Fie! thou art like one
Who standing in the fire crieth out,
Consumed by gnawing flames, and yet who
    swears
His fire burns not, though all others may,
Therefore will he not budge.   Come thou with
    me,
I have a daughter, if she liveth still,

Should have the age of her thou lovest so,

She had the name of her whom thou hast lost.

She should be beautiful; her mother was;

She should be good—I dare not think on
that.

My heart yearns toward her, and I think her
good.

I go to Rome to find her, if I can.

If she be living and be worthy thee,

As grant the gods she may, and ye can love,

When thou, more wise than I, shall have been
cured

Of this poor fever, which kills not but tortures,

Then is she thine as wife; if not as wife,'

Why then as sister; thou shalt be my son.

We'll live together, Sextus, and our world,

Ourselves alone, shall be a trinity.

SEXTUS.

I never can forget to love Salome,

Nor yet remember e'er to love another.

20*

- But I will go with thee, I'll go with thee.

Enter Herodias with chorus of attendants.

Behold the queen!

ANTONIUS.

The queen! say'st thou? the queen?

The queen I never saw—and yet—and yet—

Ye gods immortal! it is Livia!

But ah! how changed from that sweet innocent face!

Could not these fifteen years have stilled my
heart,

And with their tempests worn her image out?

And cooled my blood, whose hot steam chokes
me now?

And hardened sinews which do fail me now?

HERODIAS.

Revenged! revenged! revenged!—go to thy
place!

CHORUS.

Gone are the signs in the heavens!

Gone are the sails !

Gone is the rudder !

Tossed and beaten of waves !

Tossed and fearfully driven !

Stranded ! stranded the vessel !

HERODIAS.

Go to thy place! aha! go to thy place !

CHORUS.

Reason is whelmed by the tempest,

Light of the stars is hidden by clouds of de-
  spair !

Night cometh dark from the dreadful regions
  of madness !

HERODIAS.

Where is Salome? Ha ! I am revenged !

CHORUS.

Charmed by revenge,

Bound in its folds and writhing,

Writhing, stung and maddened to frenzy.

ANTONIUS.

Salome! ah! Salome! she's my child!

Where is she, Sextus? Fetch her, bring her
back.

Where is my child, my daughter, all my
world?

I tell thee I must have her.

SEXTUS.

              Ask the gods

To give her back; she is a vestal.

ANTONIUS.

                   No!

I'll not believe it, No! Ye gods! Ye gods!

Exhaust your thunderbolts upon my head,

Empty your quivers, send me all your plagues

In this most desolate moment of my life—

My life most desolate—swamp me with your
curses,

And in oblivion let me now forget

That ye hold curses still in store for me.—

I tell thee I will have her, Jove himself
Shall rival me in vain, she is my child;
She's all I have but curses.

SEXTUS.

Strive in vain.
She's lost to us, driven hence, herself accursed
By that arch-hatcher of conspiracies
Her mother.

ANTONIUS.

Livia again! Ye gods!
What train of curses doth he take who takes
A wanton wife! Oh! I would rather be
Chained to Prometheus's rock, my vitals eaten
By vultures daily; have my breath con-
    sumed
By noisome stench of Harpies; rather lie
With Typhon roaring under Etna's flames,
Or in the flood with Tantalus be burned
By deathless thirst, or with Ixion chained
By brazen bands upon a fiery wheel;

Rather with Sisyphus toil all my days
Than wed with such a wife, more rich in ills
Than e'er Pandora. Yet, whate'er he do
Who thus is wed, Jove, spare thy thunder-
    bolts,
He's punished in advance—and yet—and yet
I love her, Sextus; how I love her still!
The shame I feel for loving cannot drive
Love from my heart, nor can the misery
Which she hath caused me—stay, stay yet a
    space,
While I take my last look, and so sum up
My life ; then straightway will I forth with thee
To seek my child ; if we shall find her, well ;
If not, to search is all that's left me now.
And if I find her not I may find Death,
The next best, dearest friend. Ah! I was
    strong,
And while I had a daughter I was brave.
Now am I weak and have no courage left.

HERODIAS.

Toads all of them; not even food for serpents.

ANTONIUS.

Ye gods, give back my child, O give her back.

I have grown old while still in my full prime.

Look at my hair, is it not white with age?

No ill can touch me now; I am ill proof.

I could defy the power of the gods

To make me feel a curse, I'm so benumbed

With curses; and this last, so rude, so fell,

Hath changed me from a target for misfortunes

To a misfortune, and henceforth I'll go

Mixed with calamities as one of them,

Without intent and without malice cursing.

HERODIAS.

Why look'st thou so at me! Am I a sea

From which thy suns draw showers? Am 1

  the sun?

That thus thine eyes run o'er like lakes in spring

When melt the frozen snows? I am avenged '

ANTONIUS.

Nay, Livia, speak to me; know'st thou me
not?

HERODIAS.

Why, yes; thou art the witch that long ago
Stole my Antonius—nay, go thy ways.
Hast seen Antonius?—Antonius—
Who called me Livia? Ha! ha! revenged!

ANTONIUS.

Look on my face; I've seen Antonius.

HERODIAS.

Why then I pity him; thou art the beast
Which black malignity begot on folly—
Well thou resemblest on thy mother's side
Antonius, for he left me alone.

ANTONIUS.

Avenging gods! What punishment is hers!

HERODIAS.

The witch doth mutter; go thy ways, witch, go;
For I'll be damned, and be thy mistress soon,

And when I'm damned I'll burn thee, tear thy
  hair.

Yea, go thy ways, witch, go and mock me not.

SEXTUS.

The gods have mercy!—this is terrible.

HERODIAS.

Why, hush! there spoke the king of newts and
  toads.

He croaketh badly.   I've seen his majesty

I' th' mud, I' th' mud; croak me a song, good
  king,

'Tis something worse than dirge for me to die
  by.

ANTONIUS.

Ah! Livia! is this the fearful end?

HERODIAS.

End! no, 'tis the beginning; go, begone,

For thou the essence of damnation art,

And let me not be forced to swallow thee

Before my time; I'll find thee soon in Hades.

21

SEXTUS.

It is the retribution of the gods!

HERODIAS.

Thou'st seen Antonius? I know thee now.
Thou the fell fury art who drove him hence
Come back to mock me; I will pinch thee for it,
I'll pinch thee, pinch thee, pinch thee—give
    me air!

ANTONIUS.

Alas! my bleeding heart! bleed on! bleed on!

HERODIAS.

The fury whispereth; send the fury hence,
Or burn her till she bring Antonius—
I want to see him, see him ere I die.
O woe! O woe! O horror! life! O death!

CHORUS.

The dark-handed angel! The dark-handed angel!
Darkly he cometh from dark caves of life,
Lifteth the weight of humanity's burdens,
Lifteth the terrible woe of humanity,

Deepest and dimmest of mysteries

Hidden by mysteries dimmest and deepest,

Beareth man on his noiseless wings

To mysteries dimmer and deeper.

HERODIAS.

He cometh there!   I feel his fingers press

Upon my throat!—unhand me Death!—away.

CHÓRUS.

From the blissful moments, islands of bliss

Resting enchanted amid the billows of life,

Over the wavelets of time,

That cease to move for a space,

To linger upon the shores—

The shores of those islands of bliss—

Cometh thin vapor, and mists and the herald
   concealed,

Sent by the gods in mists of joy and of rapture.

HERODIAS.

To ask forgiveness—'tis a coward's act—

I'll go down cursing, and defy the gods.

CHORUS.

Noiseless he treads on the waves, nor rustle his
　　garments.

Suddenly changeth his raiment!

Blackness enshrouds him!

Billows beneath his shade grow dark and ap-
　　palling!

Lost are the islands of bliss!

Lost is the light of the skies!

Lost is the land!

Over the black waves of time,

Terrible, wildly and swiftly now rolling,

Huge and frowning and awful, the cloud of
　　death moveth.

HERODIAS.

Say, what would'st thou with me?—Ah! give
　　me air!

Revenged! I'll be upon the gods avenged!

CHORUS.

Death spreadeth darkly above thee,

Descendeth, descendeth upon thee,

Suffocating! suffocating! ah!

Joys have fled from thine arms,

Pleasures have fled,

Terror holds thee in his talons!

HERODIAS.

Thy boat! thy boat! Charon, I come! I come!

CHORUS.

Sure the justice of God,

Awfully stern its decrees;

Patience restraineth its hand

Till the day be passed, till the evening.

HERODIAS.

The fiend doth beckon me—go ye aside;

I'll in with him, and o'er the fires of hell

Brew curses for ye all—away! away!

Torment me not before my time; away!

CHORUS.

Sold in the days of its beauty and strength
    unto evil,

21*

For lust and ambition and passion and power
Lingering still upon earth,
Hideous and writhing, the soul is already with
    devils.

HERODIAS.

Ye'll chase me, will ye? ye will send me hence?
I will return and lead the damned in troops,
To be revenged on ye—nay, give me air.
The steam of hell doth choke me—give me air.

CHORUS.

Swiftly the soul approacheth its prison,
The caverns of burning remorse,
Where its impotent hate,
Despairing, shall foam with impotent ragings.

HERODIAS.

The way grows dark—devils and furies, ho !
What ! light your torches and receive your
    queen !
Let me not grope in silence down to hell,
But come with swift descent and loud acclaim.

CHORUS.

Darker and darker the way,

Fires of Hades illume not;

Night broodeth there and its light is the blackness of darkness.

Slow to the doer of evil

Seemeth his course to destruction;

Silent his thundering way and the storms that
surround him;

Fain would he hasten his steps,

Fain would he publish his infamy wider.

HERODIAS.

What! ho! up, guards of hell and seneschal!

Down with your drawbridge! Call your
warders out!

Summon your princes to their loftiest hall!

Receive your mistress as becomes her state!

CHORUS.

Watchmen watch from towers of hell forever,

Princely messengers with flaming wings invite,

Princes wait in state for proud and powerful

Weak and mean, and rich and poor alike.

Its drawbridge ever is down,

Ever its gates are open,

Ever its warders are ready.

Enemies approach not;

Dreading no foes,

It feareth no hostile invasion.

HERODIAS.

'Tis darker still; the devils then are dead,

The fires of hell are out, the furies sleep—

I'll wake them, light their fires, and send them
 forth.

Nothing in hell shall sleep when I am there.

CHORUS.

Sleepless is Evil, and sleep

Cannot abide, but fleeth in terror its presence;

Sleep is the couch of the just, at night their
 health-giving garment;

Sleep, the reward of the gods to the pure and
the gentle of spirit.

HERODIAS.

I come! I come! world, for a space, good-night
Hail! Pluto, hail! infernal horrors! hail!

Dies.

CHORUS.

Thus, alone and revengeful and raging,
Goeth the soul to blackest perdition,
When the gods are despised and contemned,
When their servants are mocked and abused. ˙

ANTONIUS.

So farewell, Livia, alas! alas!

CHORUS.

From the vast and the dim, the hall of his star-
pillared palace,
Steppeth the sun in his strength; he taketh
his bow and his quiver.
Filled is his quiver with days, and bound together with ages.

Light from his locks he is shaking ; he girdeth
    mists flaming about him.
Taketh an arrowy day and bendeth his bow
    the electric.
Swiftly, gleaming with light, the shaft skim
    the airy abysses,
Flashing it quivereth in earth, and sheddeth
    its light o'er the waters.
Night, benignant with shade, and with dewy
    balm and with slumber,
Cometh on silent wing and draweth the light-
    giving arrow,
Wrappeth the earth in its shade and cooleth
    the wound and the fever,
Placeth the languishing earth in oblivion
    sweetly to slumber.
So from the light-giving hand of the mighty
    Creator, Life-Giver,
Speedeth the arrowy life, and quiv'reth in
    man for a season ;

So doth benignant Death draw forth the fiery
    arrow,
Giveth the longed-for repose—and wrappeth
    man in its shadow.

THE END.

www.ingramcontent.com/pod-product-compliance
Lightning Source LLC
Chambersburg PA
CBHW020057030726
47498CB00006B/1826